# Starch and Strategy

A Variation on *Pride and Prejudice*

and *Persuasion*

## Corrie Garrett

Lanmon Books

MORGANTOWN, WEST VIRGINIA

Lanmon Books
28 Amherst Rd.
Morgantown, WV 26505
www.lanmonbooks.com

Publisher's Note: This is a work of fiction. Names, characters, places, and incidents are a product of the author's imagination. Locales and public names are sometimes used for atmospheric purposes. Any resemblance to actual people, living or dead, or to businesses, companies, events, institutions, or locales is completely coincidental.

Book Layout ©2017 BookDesignTemplates.com

Starch and Strategy/ Corrie Garrett. -- 1st ed.
ISBN: 979-8-88914-004-7

*To Mr. Collins, Caroline Bingley, Lady Catherine, and all the other P&P characters we love to hate, who make the book such a delight to read.*

## { 1 }

THIS IS AN ASSORTMENT OF HORRORS and no mistake," Caroline Bingley whispered to Mr. Darcy. "If Lydia Bennet's wild energy does not abate soon, I expect to see her swinging from those dreadful green drapes like a monkey. Furthermore, Lady Lucas has described no less than three bruised and broken toes to me in *excruciating* detail."

"Please don't share the recital with me," Darcy said. He took a swig of cold punch, and his eyes followed Miss Lizzy Bennet as she danced down the line with her partner.

"I see you wince at the refreshment," Caroline said, "and I do not blame you. Even Charles made a face at it, though I could not bring him to admit what was wrong."

"The brandy was left open too long, the lemons were overripe, and there is far too much sugar." Darcy grimaced. "It tastes like they were trying to satisfy Prinny's sweet tooth."

Caroline laughed, but they were interrupted by a dowdy young gentleman wearing the collar of a clergyman.

"Excuse me," he said. "Do I have the honor of addressing Mr. Fitzwilliam Darcy, nephew of the most generous and respected Lady Catherine de Bourgh?"

Caroline curled her lip, anticipating Darcy's setdown to this little toady.

Darcy swallowed, still clearing the sugary punch from his teeth, and he merely inclined his head. "Yes, sir."

"What a fine thing this is," the man exclaimed. "But I do not know why I am surprised, for I must tell you that I have had many fine coincidences in my life. I consider them the blessings of a most beneficent Providence, and also—partly!—the reward of my own poor efforts! For you must allow that the happy circumstances which have placed us at the same ball would still have been unnoticed if I had not sought you out." He smiled with great complacency and self-importance.

Caroline could not help the small sound of scorn and disbelief that escaped her. Who was this pompous man with baggy knees to his pantaloons and a disastrous,

Stanhope-inspired haircut to address Mr. Darcy this way?

"Yet we are all at sea as to this great occurrence," Caroline said, "for you have not identified yourself. I do not say *introduce*, for that would require a mutual friend."

"Ah, of course. My cousin Elizabeth did not feel herself well-enough acquainted with you to perform an introduction, but I am a man of the cloth and do not bow to the whims of females. I am Mr. William Collins, and I have the extreme good fortune to hold the living of Rosings Park. Indeed, I live almost within sight of the beautiful facade of Rosings!"

Caroline was sure Mr. Darcy had his measure now. He opened his mouth, hopefully to utter one of his withering set-downs, but the man cut him off.

"You honored aunt, Lady Catherine, had me to dinner only last week—the veal cutlets were dressed with her own recipe for white sauce, quite delicious!—and I can inform you that she was in excellent health when last I left her." He sucked his teeth and smiled up at them again. "And now I can tell her that her beloved nephew is also in good health." He lowered his eyes for a frank assessment, his eyes cataloging Mr. Darcy's polished dancing shoes, his evening wear of dove gray pantaloons, white shirt, and deep blue superfine evening coat. "You are well, are you not, sir?"

Darcy wrinkled his nose at this unsubtle assessment "Not as well as I was two minutes ago."

Mr. Collins showed not the slightest understanding of this. "That is unfortunate. It may be the heat of the rooms, or perhaps the rather—ahem—pungent quality of the punch. Lady Catherine considers that any more than a pound of sugar is vulgar and extravagant."

"It is the company," Darcy said baldly. He bowed to the man and turned away.

Caroline looked over her shoulder as they made their way around the edge of the room. "He still does not understand you. He glares about as if someone else was annoying you. What a self-important piece of buffoonery!"

Darcy sighed. "Shall we dance? It is loud and unpleasant, but at least we cannot be accosted on the dance floor."

Caroline felt a glow of satisfaction that he was turning to her. The sound of *we* on his lips was something she had long wished to hear.

The Darcy family was proud and old, and Mr. Darcy was just as proud as his lineage deserved. No London dowager would sneer at Miss Bingley and her family if she became the new Mrs. Darcy.

They entered the floor when one of the guests who'd appointed himself the unofficial caller, began to loudly proclaim the steps of the next dance. It was a country dance, and Mr. Darcy looked none too pleased. Caroline schooled her face to bland disinterest as well. Everyone knew only provincials enjoyed a country dance.

Unfortunately, Miss Lizzy Bennet joined the set in the next position to them. Her partner was a local boy who still had spots. Mr. Darcy spent the first quarter of the dance looking at Lizzy, and Caroline felt more than a bit galled by it.

Worse, when the dance broke into foursomes, and the next step called for the dancers to circle with their diagonal partner, Caroline got the spotted youth, and Lizzy got Mr. Darcy.

Double worse, Lizzy's sister Lydia was in the next foursome, and she skipped so exuberantly, clapping her hands so wildly, that she gave Caroline a sharp kick in the calf.

Lydia laughed at the collision. "Sorry!" she called as she and her partner fell back to the bottom of the lines.

Caroline grimaced, ending the dance with less than her usual grace because her leg hurt. "What an odious monkey," she whispered to Darcy when he placed his right hand against hers.

The corner of his mouth twitched, and Caroline was rewarded for the small bruise the youngest Bennet sister had given her.

When their group had completed the prime set, they fell back to the bottom of the lines. Mr. Darcy and the youth stood on the men's side, she and Lizzy on the women's.

Now Caroline's brother Charles was in the prime position with Jane, along with Miss Elliot and one of the officers.

Her brother was oblivious to everything but Jane. Charles was exasperating; he got besotted the same way any bricklayer or stable hand would, without reserve or caution. Truly elegant affection, Caroline believed, would never be so all-consuming.

While Miss Bingley barely tolerated the insipidly sweet Jane Bennet and disdained Lizzy, Lydia, and the others, she was rather in approval of the Elliot sisters. Their father was a baronet, and though the three young ladies were very different from one another, they all had a dignity and poise that spoke for itself.

The eldest Miss Elliot was the finest by far. She was dressed in the latest French fashions, with braided sleeves and intricate lace over an underdress of dashing cerulean blue. She and Caroline had had a satisfying conversation about bodices, and the exigencies of private country balls. Miss Elliot was the epitome of a lady born to wealth, status, and beauty. Her coloring was quite similar to Caroline's own.

The younger two sisters were also pretty, though not as striking as their older sister. There was Miss Anne Elliot, who was about Miss Bingley's own age and had had very little to say during the conversation. Her hair was darker, her manner reserved. She was inattentive until Bingley and Darcy chanced to mention the naval action near Gibraltar. She was deeply knowledgeable about the navy.

The youngest sister was Miss Mary Elliot, only eighteen. She had sat down after only two dances, declaring that she twisted her ankle so badly she might have broken it, although this dire statement was completely disregarded by her family. She was a trifle shrill, but a far sight more genteel than the Bennet girls. She didn't flirt outrageously, laugh loudly, or kick anyone when she danced.

Their father, Sir Walter Elliot, was also a fine-looking man for his age. In fact, as Caroline's dance with Mr. Darcy ended, Miss Elliot and her father approached them.

"My dear Miss Bingley, allow me to introduce my father, Sir Walter Elliot. Father, this is Miss Bingley and Mr. Darcy, several of those visiting from London, as I told you. Of all the people here, I believe they are the least likely to perturb you."

"You are a good-looking man," said Sir Walter to Darcy, "and that is a *relief*, for I never knew how ugly Hertfordshire had become. I was here in my youth and there were never so many lined foreheads, puffed chins, and blotched cheeks. It is depressing."

Caroline laughed, and Sir Walter turned to her. "I am always pleased to meet a friend of my dear Elizabeth. She often has friends with us at Kellynch Hall, though not so of late." He grimaced at someone over her shoulder. "Lady Lucas is approaching, and I do not like her hairline. Will you dance with me, Miss Bingley? Though I am a widower, I am not so old nor so infirm as to preclude dancing."

Miss Bingley would have danced with far worse had a baronet offered, and thankfully Sir Walter was quite handsome. "I would be honored, sir, as any lady in the room would be."

"Now that is well put and promptly said. I would that Anne had a little of that wit and quickness!"

Darcy watched, bemused, as Sir Walter led Miss Bingley toward the impromptu dance floor of Lucas Lodge.

He had now been visually examined and appraised by two gentlemen in less than five minutes. What an unpleasant thing country parties were! Darcy was used to ignoring attention from women in London, but Mr. Collins's and Sir Walter's comments on his physique caught him unprepared. Where was his greatcoat when he needed it?

Miss Elliot waited next to him, perhaps expecting him to ask her to dance.

She was to be disappointed. He never let social pressure influence him to dance when he did not care to, and he did not know Miss Elliot. He preferred to dance with those he was acquainted with.

"Are you enjoying Hertfordshire?" she asked.

"It is tolerable. I am happy to help my friend get settled, though I look forward to returning to Derbyshire."

"Yes, to Pemberley, of course! I have seen its entry in the *Guide Book to Derbyshire and the North*. You will have seen a similar entry about our home. Kellynch Hall is in the Elliot entry in *The Baronetage.*"

Mr. Darcy inclined his head. "Perhaps I have." He had no recollection of Kellynch Hall, but then he had plenty to do with the Pemberley estate since his parents' death. He did not devote much time to studying guidebooks. He certainly never wasted time pouring over *The Baronetage*, which was merely a description of those who purchased titles from King Charles II.

Darcy could easily purchase a baronetcy for himself, as the only stipulation was that one's estate supplied a thousand pounds a year in income. Mr. Darcy's estates, both at Pemberley and elsewhere, produced far more than that. He wasn't interested in buying a title, however. His father had died a mere Mr. Darcy, and he would die as Mr. Darcy also.

Miss Elliot looked toward the dancers, but Mr. Darcy refused to take the hint.

"Please excuse me," he said.

He moved around to the north end of the room, where the crush was a bit less. The Lucases were no doubt amiable people, but they overcrowded their rooms. A third of the families might have been left off the invitation list.

Miss Elizabeth Bennet was also sitting out this dance, and she rested on a bench near the wall with her friend Miss Lucas, the eldest daughter of the house.

"This shelf nonsense is ridiculous," Lizzy was saying to her friend, in answer to something she'd said. "Why should a woman be less desirable when she has maturity, sense, and experience behind her? *On the shelf,* what an ugly phrase. You make yourself sound like a blackberry jam."

"Unfortunately, men don't propose for maturity and sense," Miss Lucas said. "You are too idealistic, Lizzy."

"Perhaps, but I am not at all naïve; I know how absurd people are. But look, there is the eldest Miss Elliot, who is the same age as you, if not a year or so older, and she does not expect anything less than adoration."

"She has wealth and looks," Miss Lucas said, though not harshly.

"True, though I wonder if she works *The Baronetage* into every conversation or if that was merely a lucky coincidence with me."

Mr. Darcy found himself smiling.

Lizzy's eyes flickered to him and when he made eye contact, flickered away.

She turned back to her friend, leaning close. "What does Mr. Darcy mean by listening to me again?"

Miss Lucas smiled. "You did say you would challenge him on it next time."

"So I did!" Lizzy at once turned to him. "Do you not think I am correct, sir, that the social custom which considers women over a certain age to be less desirable is antiquated? Does it not encourage men—even men of sense—to first look among the youngest and least mature of his acquaintances?"

"I don't think a man of sense should offer for a silly woman whatever her age."

"Perhaps they should not, but they often do."

"Then I do not think the case is helped by choosing an older woman; I do not think that age alone improves a person in character or intelligence. The use of the intervening years is the deciding factor, and far too few women of my acquaintance use their time well."

Lizzy found herself reluctantly agreeing with this perspective. Her mother was an excellent example of a lady whose passing years—spent gossiping and daydreaming about the prospects of her five daughters—had given her a certain shrewdness, but no improvement in sense, tact, or good-humor.

"But you must admit," Lizzy argued anyway, "that there is a better chance of a woman of seven-and-twenty having sense and maturity than a girl of seventeen, though neither is guaranteed."

"I can concede that much."

Did his eyes find Lydia as she danced and flirted with another officer, or was that only Lizzy's paranoia? Surely not everyone could be as painfully aware of her family's flaws as she was.

"That is settled then." Lizzy would have walked away, taking Charlotte with her, but Charlotte's father stopped them. His rich green coat contrasted rather sharply with the redness of his cheeks and nose.

"What a fine evening, Mr. Darcy! I was happy to see you dance with Miss Bingley, and I hope you will dance again. Dancing is one of the finest refinements of polished society, I think."

"It is also a popular pastime in less polished circles. Most savages dance."

"What an amusing thought!"

Lizzy glared reprovingly at Mr. Darcy. Sir William might not recognize an insult when he heard one, but she did.

Unfortunately, her persistent cousin, Mr. Collins, chose that moment to join their small group as well.

"My dear Miss Elizabeth, will you not join me for a turn?" he said. "Though I am a clergyman, I find no harm in dancing. Lady Catherine—" he bowed to Mr. Darcy, "finds it a perfectly acceptable mode of exercise! The movement of the feet, so lively, even if one misses half the steps! It is also invigorating to one's heart and skin. Come dance with me."

"Oh, I—I suppose I have no excuse not to."

Mr. Collins laughed. "Such modesty."

Lizzy sighed. Another who did not understand insults.

She accidentally caught Mr. Darcy's eye again, and she correctly read his look of displeasure. Lizzy was annoyed. If he thought so poorly of her cousin and herself—which of course he did, having called her "barely tolerable" that first night—he need not follow her about on subsequent evenings to mock her.

Lizzy joined the dance with Mr. Collins. They'd completed only one call before he stepped on her foot. Her dancing slippers were not reinforced, and she swallowed a whimper.

He apologized, of course, but was not listening to the caller and so followed with a *Chasse setting step* instead of a *traveling step*. She had to pull him into the next position, and his apology interrupted the *jete assembly*, when they all ought to have jumped and landed on two feet facing inward. He tried to land on his left foot and wobbled ominously toward poor Miss Mary Elliot until Lizzy steadied him.

The next portion of the dance was fine, a series of regular *allemande* drop steps, which even he could do, but then it went into a simple *chasse*, and he stepped on her foot again.

Lizzy found the entire dance a punishment beyond what even she had anticipated. She resolutely refused to dance again, and she avoided Mr. Darcy's satirical gaze.

MISS BINGLEY LENT ONE ARM on her escritoire and considered the note before her.

She did not particularly want to invite Jane Bennet to Netherfield, but the note was written, and the ink was almost dry.

Jane was pretty and sweet, but she was not very interesting. She did not know much about the latest fashions, and what knowledge she had was from outdated copies of the *Ladies' Bazaar.* Jane knew none of Miss Bingley's London friends and had no gossip of note to impart. She liked music but did not play much. She liked art but did not draw much.

Miss Bingley ripped the note up and threw the pieces in the fire. Though it was only October, it was a cold, gray day, and the fire was welcome.

She composed another note, this one to the eldest of the Elliot sisters.

*Dear Miss Elliot,*

*I know you are visiting friends who have a stronger claim on you and your family than I can do, but I beg a visit. I am alone today, for my brother and his friend dine with the officers, and I am dreadfully dull. Do please visit me at Netherfield Park. Either or both of your sisters are also welcome, though I do not know if your excellent father would like to spare you all at once.*

*Yours sincerely,*
*Caroline Bingley*

Some two hours later, even though it began to pour rain soon after she dispatched her note, the Elliot coach arrived. It was a fine vehicle, of the latest mode, with the Elliot coat of arms brightly imprinted on the door in red, yellow, and black.

It was not only Miss Elliot who disembarked, but her father and youngest sister also. Soon they were ushered into the drawing room.

"We have presumed upon your hospitality to bring my father as well!" Miss Elliot said. "I assured him that it would not be an imposition. You are everything gracious, so we are here as you see."

"On the contrary, I am honored to have you all to visit. A very pleasant surprise."

"Well, not Anne," Miss Elliot corrected, "but Anne never goes anywhere she doesn't have to. She is sulking because she says we ought to have stayed through October to visit our tenants after the harvest or some such thing. She is frightfully dour when she does not get her way, but we do not let her moods affect us."

Sir Walter looked about the room and found a mirror. He placed himself before it and fixed a lock of hair that had been blown askew when he got out of the carriage. "Yes, we do appreciate your hospitality. I have been acquainted with Sir William Lucas these twenty years, since he was knighted, but the years have not been kind. It is difficult for one of my sensibility to sit with him amid the wreck of his former good looks."

"I'm sure it must be," Caroline agreed. "I have only met him this past month and also find it difficult."

Mary Elliot shuddered. "The Lucas children are loud and tiresome, and there are so *many* of them. I have had the headache today, and though Miss Charlotte Lucas told the children to be quiet, they did not even *pretend* to do so. I suffer dreadfully on visits, and no one sympathizes." She plopped down on a chaise and half-closed her eyes.

"That would be tiring," Caroline said. "I find all the families in Hertfordshire to be sadly loud."

Mary opened her eyes again. "It is not so in Somerset. Our friends the Musgroves also have many children, but Mrs. Musgrove keeps them away. Except for Henrietta and Louisa, of course, for they are only two years younger than me."

Miss Elliot scoffed, taking a seat. "The Musgrove offspring are obnoxious, Mary, but Henrietta and Louisa idolize us, that is why you like them."

Sir Walter removed a speck of white from his morning coat of pale yellow. "Charles Musgrove is growing to be a tolerably good-looking young man; we suspect he will offer for Anne or Mary. The Musgroves are not a titled family, but they are the most important family in the district, barring ourselves. It would not be an untoward match for one of them."

Miss Elliot shook her head. "We must cease talking of persons Miss Bingley does not know; she cannot be interested. Tell me, are you familiar with Somerset?"

"A little with Bath, yes," said Caroline. "And Wells Cathedral is magnificent."

"Ah, Wells!" said Sir Walter. "Yes, one can generally count on meeting a titled visitor or two during the warm parts of the year. I always take visitors from Kellynch to Wells Cathedral."

"The scissor arches are extraordinary," Caroline said. "And the north face quite takes one to the Dark Ages. I revere Gothic architecture."

Miss Elliot yawned. "Yes, it is all the rage, I suppose. It is not very modern."

Caroline could converse knowledgeably on a number of subjects, architecture included, but Miss Elliot was not much interested. Caroline changed the subject. "I have heard that Somerset possesses the deepest gorge in England, though I have not seen it."

"Oh, you mean the Cheddar Gorge," Mary put in, not opening her eyes. "It is very dreary to get there, the path shakes one to the bone."

"I don't like the cheese they make there," Sir Walter added. "Cheddar cheese will never catch on. It is too sharp for the sophisticated palate."

That was all that was to be said about the gorge, so Caroline pressed on. "Do you go to Bath often? That must be relatively near your estate."

"Yes, sometimes," Miss Elliot said. "Anne hates it; she is so moody when we take her. I suppose it is because she was at school there."

Mary shrugged. "I was at school there until last year, and *I* do not hate it. Furthermore, my school years were ever so much worse than Anne's, for my health is not good. None of the teachers sympathized but merely told me I could not always feel faint when I got low marks. As if I cared anything for their ridiculous requirements! The only pleasant things were the walks, when one could see the dandies going to the pump room."

Miss Elliot took a turn in front of the mirror. "You ought not to talk so, Mary. Dandies! Next you will have your heart turned by these officers."

Sir Walter raised his hands in horror. "But no, my dear, do not put it in her head. They are all so weathered from their campaigns in France and in the north, they are frightful. Only the navy is worse for red-noses. Mary can do much better than an army officer."

"I must agree," Caroline said. "The daughters of Sir Walter can look as high as they wish."

"Thank you," he said, gratified. "You see the world as it is, which I cannot say for all young ladies. Anne told me only yesterday that if we do not retrench, she fears she and her sisters may give up finding good husbands! Can you imagine? As if the Elliot name has no value!"

"I fear every family has one member with such misplaced humility," said Caroline. "My own brother, though an excellent man in every respect, does not value himself or his family as he ought. I suspect he would lose his heart to any country miss who laughed with him."

Sir Walter shook his head. "That is serious, and you must do what you can to dissuade him. He is a handsome young man, your brother, even though he has no title. He ought to marry a wealthy, beautiful woman.

There are so many ugly children, I declare it a *crime* to make more of them."

The long and short of the day was that, by the time Bingley and Darcy returned, Caroline had invited the Elliots to stay at Netherfield Park, rather than the crowded environs of Lucas Lodge.

Mr. Bingley immediately seconded this offer. "Why, quite, sir, we would be honored to have you. Any of Caroline's friends are welcome, and I hope you will consider me a friend as well. The more the merrier!"

Sir Walter, who had had time to appreciate the spaciousness of Netherfield, its many mirrors, and his own importance therein, agreed to grace them with his presence with great affability.

He even said, when Caroline stood with Miss Elliot to walk them out, "I declare, you are as like as two peas in a pod! And I cannot give a higher compliment than that, Miss Bingley, for my eldest is clearly the beauty of the family."

The worst of it, Darcy decided three days later, when the Elliots were settled in Netherfield, was not Sir Walter's vanity, though it was immense, or Miss Elliot's interest in him, though it was blatant, but that they made Caroline worse.

Darcy did not have an extremely close relationship with Bingley's sister, but he considered her to be a friend. He didn't plan to marry her, but he could do worse. The Bingleys were not an old family, and their fortune came from trade a generation back, but that did not weigh with him. He was not obsessed with titles like Sir Walter, and he did not care about a woman's family connections as long as they were well-bred, distant, or dead.

Caroline was intelligent, and he could have an interesting conversation with her about art, music, architecture, or even politics. But with the Elliots, she seemed to regress to their level. Sir Walter thought of little beside his own appearance and that of others; Caroline flattered him. Miss Elliot thought of little besides herself, her importance, and her father; Caroline encouraged her. Miss Mary Elliot thought of little besides her own aches and (imagined?) pains; Caroline sympathized.

Darcy wanted to throw them out of the house, but Bingley resisted. "They're not so bad as all that!"

"I admit Miss Anne seems sensible, and Caroline has enjoyed playing duets with her, but she barely speaks otherwise. The others—" Darcy shuddered.

"They're a little proud, to be sure, but not nearly so bad as your Aunt Cather—" Bingley broke off and coughed something. "Never mind. They don't intimidate me, and Caroline likes 'em."

Darcy sighed. "That is fair, and it is your own house. I suppose if I do not like the company, I ought to take myself off."

"No, don't do that! I still haven't decided whether I ought to buy this place. The house is fine, but I know I'll need to bring the tenancies up to par, and some of the tenants look mean."

"Don't be childish, Charles. If you need to get rid of a lay-about tenant, you simply evict them when their lease is up."

"That is easy for you to say! You are so tall, you have only to stand near someone and glare, and they will clear out. People argue with me."

"Don't let them."

Bingley threw up his hands. "You simply do not understand. And then there are the hovels some of them live in. If I own the estate, I'm responsible to improve them, am I not? I need to calculate if I'll have enough to bring this place into good repair."

This was one of the reasons Darcy liked Bingley. Bingley's fortune might be new, but he had a better heart for dependents than many a landed aristocrat like Sir Walter. Bingley, when he bought an estate, would take good care of his land and workers and tenants.

"All right, I'll stay and help you calculate the needed investment," Darcy said.

"I knew you would." Bingley smiled a little self-consciously. "Care to accompany me on a morning call?"

Darcy took a deep breath through his nose. "Your diligence to duty is remarkable."

"Come, Darcy! All work and no play, you know, it's not healthy."

"You're very far from such a problem."

"Yet you bear with me somehow."

"Is it to be the Lucases or the Longs?"

Bingley huffed. "You know very well I meant the Bennets; you needn't tease me."

At the Bennets, they found several officers also visiting, their red coats and regimentals making the room as visually assaulting as it was auditorily overpowering.

Darcy examined the room, picked up a newspaper, and sat on a lone chair to the right of the hearth. It was a little too warm, but from here he could hear Lizzy's conversation without being obvious or being constantly accosted by others.

He did not intend to raise false hopes in Miss Elizabeth Bennet (or in any young lady for that matter) by acting in an interested manner. However, he couldn't deny that she was more enjoyable to listen to and look at than any other lady of the neighborhood.

She was speaking to one of the older officers, a Colonel Forster.

"But are these continued removals difficult for Mrs. Forster? For you must go wherever the army sends you." Lizzy was not so finely dressed as she had been at Lucas Lodge, and her hair looked as if she had gone for a walk and not tidied it after. She was still distractingly pretty, and her eyes missed nothing.

"Difficult to move?" Colonel Forster said. "My wife likes it more than me, if you can believe that! She's always happy to explore a new town. She says the orders always come just when she is getting bored and ready to move! No, it is my old bones that protest an unfamiliar bed at the end of the day."

"Old! You say it so I will contradict you, but you are caught out, for I never pander to such obvious leads."

"Not even to buoy the spirits of a poor old soldier, tasked with whipping thirty green officers into shape by the end of the month?" He laughed. "You cannot be so hard-hearted."

"I have just such a hard heart, and I am confident that you already know you are neither poor nor old."

The Colonel laughed again and moved away to another group. "Miss Kitty must cheer me, then; she always does!"

Lizzy smiled at his back, but then she realized Darcy was looking at her instead of his newspaper. "Again you are listening, sir! Do you mean to make me paranoid in your presence?"

Darcy looked back at his paper, then back at her. "Not at all. You and the Colonel grabbed my attention. You don't fancy a military life?"

"Not for itself. I have lived in Longbourn my entire life. I'm not sure I'd know how to go on without putting down roots. However, I daresay I should change my mind if the right person offered, for so many girls do, and I don't claim to be stronger than the rest of my sex."

"You don't plan to live in Hertfordshire forever, though, surely?"

"Perhaps not, though I would not mind it. I plan to be the most excellent aunt imaginable to my future nieces and nephews. I suppose I will split the year between my sisters. I'll be the old maid Aunt Lizzy, come to care for the children and batten off their households."

Darcy's mouth twitched. "Now you are doing what you accused Colonel Forster of. You declare that you will never marry to get me to contradict you."

The revulsion of her expression startled him. "That was *not* my aim; you misunderstand me. Excuse me, sir."

Lizzy rose and joined her sister Mary at the pianoforte, putting herself out of range of conversation.

Hm. Darcy did not think worse of her for her slight outburst. He appreciated that she was not on the catch for him, and she did look genuinely startled. Really, he ought not to have teased her. It was dangerously close to flirting, and he did *not* want to raise false hopes. That would be unkind to any young lady, and more so to one he respected.

It was a pity about her family. Be she ever so appealing, to marry anyone whose immediate family was so vulgar and pushing was unthinkable. It was for the best she had not taken him seriously.

Lizzy felt nearly ill as she sat by Mary at the pianoforte and listened to her complain about the company.

That the arrogant Mr. Darcy should think Lizzy was *flirting* with him—trying to trip him into talking of marriage—ugh! She rejected the thought violently.

Her friends here in Hertfordshire were used to hearing her talk so and did not think anything of it. The more she replayed the conversation, she realized it *had* sounded like flirting—that was even worse! It was her fault for mentioning being a perpetual aunt.

Her mother told her often that her lively tongue would get her in trouble, and she was right.

"These people won't stop talking long enough for me to play anything," Mary griped. "It is too provoking."

She left the piano bench, only to be replaced by Mr. Collins.

"Miss Elizabeth, my sweet cousin, I notice that you also feel the press of the room to be too much. You will be happy to know that Lady Catherine never over fills her drawing room. It is, of course, a much larger room than this—meaning no disrespect to you!—but even so, she rarely has more than seven or eight persons to dine. I, myself, as I have told you, am invited weekly. *Weekly.*" His voice was almost in her ear as he leaned toward her to be heard. The warmth of his breath hit her neck.

"Yes. You have told me several times." Lizzy was too annoyed with herself to use tact with Mr. Collins. He had switched his amorous attention from Jane to her, and she could not dissuade him. "And I believe I must tell you, for I cannot pretend to be blind to your pref- erence, that I should be a wretched parson's wife. I am flighty, and stubborn, and—and impulsive. I am not ig- norant of the honor you seek to offer me, but it really is not in your best interest."

He tittered. "So modest! So dissembling! I am glad that you are not the sort to be *pushing*, and I am certain Lady Catherine will be pleased with your personal hu- mility."

"I am not being arch or coy or even humble. I do not particularly wish to meet Lady Catherine."

Even this direct attack was useless. "You must not be scared, my dear cousin. Perhaps in my gratitude and appreciation for her ladyship's condescension to me, I have given you the impression that she is too exacting, too refined for you. It is not so! She is of such genteel blood, of such condescension, that she is *never* above her company. She converses with the chicken man as easily as the gentry! Why, I heard her only a month ago giving the groom a recipe for her own poultice for drawing pus!"

"Admirable." Lizzy rose from the bench. Was she surrounded by men who believed she wanted them? Though loath to interrupt Jane and Bingley, Lizzy approached them out of desperation. They were a little apart by the window, ostensibly watching the geese on the small pond that could be seen down the hill.

"You and your sister must come visit us tomorrow," Charles was saying. "The dreadful rain has finally stopped, and I know Caroline would be happy to have you. I'll remind her to send a note."

"Please don't feel you must," Jane said. "We heard from the Lucases that you are hosting Sir Walter Elliot and his daughters. I am sure your dear sister has all the company she needs at present."

"Caroline? Nonsense! She delights in company. In town, we're never alone from one evening to the next." He turned to Lizzy. "You will support me, will you not?"

"In anything, at any time," Lizzy said.

He laughed. "Excellent! But no, now I feel guilty, for I have not earned such loyalty."

Lizzy was interrupted by Lydia, who shouted across the room, "I say, Mr. Bingley! You will give that ball, soon, will you not? I am utterly dependent on it! I have told all my friends, and the officers declare it is all a take-in. Prove them wrong!"

"Lydia, you cannot *demand* a ball—" Lizzy began.

"But I say that she can," said Mr. Bingley, "For it is of all things what I should like, too." He leaned closer to Jane. "Will you save the first dance for me, please?"

Jane smiled up at him. "Yes, of course."

As Mr. Bingley and Mr. Darcy took their leave, Lizzy and Jane accompanied them into the vestibule, past the library door where their father hid, and out into the side yard where their groom would bring their horses out. Lizzy knew she ought to leave well enough alone, but she couldn't bear to leave Mr. Darcy with the impression that she was chasing him.

It was intolerable that a woman could not say a true thing and be believed. Unfortunately, she could not merely blurt out the truth—it would sound as if she "protest too much," like Hamlet's mother in the play.

Luckily, Mr. Bingley came to her rescue. "You will enjoy our ball also, won't you, Miss Elizabeth? I know that you like to dance almost as much as me, though Darcy will complain about it."

"I do not complain," Darcy said. "I observe."

"You should not push your friend to dance," Lizzy said to Bingley. "He will probably end up with a partner he finds barely tolerable, and it will be all your fault."

Darcy shot a quick, understanding look at her.

Jane looked quite shocked. "I'm sure he wouldn't— that is, I'm sure we will all have a lovely evening. Please give my greetings to Caroline."

When they had gone, Jane gave Lizzy as stern a glance as she could muster. "That was *not* kind, Lizzy. He ought not to have commented on you like that, but we do not know the circumstances. It could be that he is already sorry, and to rub his face in it is not well done! Indeed, I believe he *is* sorry, for he has made a point to talk to you at the Lucases and at our home. He likes you!"

"No, he doesn't. He just lurks nearby listening until I talk to him."

Jane gave a smug smile, at least as smug as her compassion allowed. "Charlotte agrees with me. Either way, he wanted to talk to you."

"You make him sound nicer than he is."

"I only know that he looked very self-conscious and sorry just now. You ought not try to embarrass anyone in front of their friends."

"I wish you will tell Lydia that. She seems to *delight* in embarrassing me in front of my friends."

Lizzy's mood improved at her Aunt Phillips's supper that evening. The Elliot girls were present, but Mr. Bingley and Mr. Darcy were not, thankfully.

Her aunt had invited many of the officers, and several were new to the neighborhood. One man in particular, a Mr. Wickham, was much noticed by the ladies for his fine figure and handsome face.

He approached Lizzy, with a gratifying look of admiration and, as they chatted, an instant feeling of camaraderie.

Sadly for her, he was distracted by several of the Miss Elliots. Soon he was seated next to the youngest, Mary Elliot, who seemed to have entirely forgotten how ill she'd felt that morning. The attention of a handsome and charming officer was an effective and well-known cure.

Lizzy laughed it off, though she had the vague feeling that the night could have gone very differently, if Mr. Wickham had sat down next to *her* instead of Miss Mary.

# { 3 }

CAROLINE WAS COERCED INTO INVITING Jane and Lizzy Bennet for a luncheon visit; there was no other way to put it.

Charles was in general the most easy-going of brothers, but he could at times get a fixed idea and refuse to leave it, like a schoolboy. Or a puppy.

Caroline spent the morning in Netherfield's main drawing room, the one which also contained the pianoforte. Anne Elliot played the instrument, and Caroline brought her embroidery in to enjoy it.

"You play very well," Caroline said. "You sound like you have had the advantage of a London master."

"No." Anne's fingers continued moving. "I was at school in Bath. We had a very good instructor, though I believe he was from Surrey. I was missing my mother, and I used my lessons as a distraction."

Caroline's gaze went to the middle distance. "My mother died when I was twelve. I don't think she could play, but she wanted us—Louisa and I—to be proficient."

"What was her name?"

"Elaine." Caroline coughed and smoothed a stray hair off a cushion. "She would hardly believe where we are now. Charles buying an estate. A baronet staying with us. She always wanted us to better ourselves."

"I'm sure she would be proud of you." Anne continued with her music.

Caroline wondered if Anne was truly as moody and difficult as Miss Elliot described, or if it was only family prejudice. It was a pity Anne was not prettier. She almost looked as if she could be, but her skin was pale and there were circles under her eyes. Those eyes were slightly red-rimmed, and her arms looked scrawny and blotchy as she played, instead of having any pleasing roundness.

Her hair was not bad, being a shiny dark brown, but she dressed it in flat bands that did nothing for her silhouette. She looked faded, and rather tired.

"Do you look forward to the Little Season this year?" Caroline asked when Anne finished her song.

"No. I don't go to London if I can help it," Anne said. "There isn't anything for me there."

"Oh, yes, your father did tell me that there was a young man in your region who was dangling after you. A Charles Musgrove?" This was Caroline's best attempt at friendliness, an offer to let Anne gossip, preen, or complain.

Instead, Anne only grew paler and folded her hands. "No."

Caroline blinked. No, there was no young man? Or no, he wasn't dangling after her? That was a comprehensive snub when Caroline was only trying to be *kind*.

Anne winced. "That is—My father's expectations are not always accurate."

Caroline shrugged. "You needn't talk about it if you don't wish to."

"I don't, thank you." Anne took herself away.

Moody, indeed!

Caroline was soon joined by Anne's sisters. Miss Elliot was dressed again in the highest fashion, quite different from the outmoded gown that Anne had worn. Even Mary, the youngest, was not as well-dressed as her eldest sister.

It was not a mystery. Their father, Sir Walter, made no secret that Elizabeth was his favorite. Caroline could not blame him; Elizabeth was clever and elegant, but they did seem a trifle harsh to the younger two. Caroline's own father, who had survived his wife a decade before succumbing to an inflammation of the stomach, had been doting with all three children.

He had a special place for Charles, of course, as his son and heir, but he had been quite affectionate with herself and Louisa.

Miss Elliot sat down at the pianoforte and picked out a tune. She clearly did not play and soon grew frustrated.

"Stupid instrument." She turned away. "Does it always rain this much in Hertfordshire? It is so cold and windy and wet."

"I think all of England could be described that way."

Miss Elliot frowned. "Still. Where has your brother gone today? Will he return soon? I am bored."

"I understand completely," Caroline said, "and they will return soon. Charles convinced me to invite the elder two Bennet girls today. That will—er—enliven us all, I'm sure."

"Which two are the eldest?" Miss Elliot demanded.

"The sweet, pretty one and the skinny, impertinent one."

Miss Elliot smirked. "I know exactly what you mean."

"How would you describe *us*?" Mary asked. "If people asked?"

Caroline blushed. "I probably ought not attempt it."

She knew her brother would not appreciate the way she'd just described the Bennets. Furthermore, the words that came to mind for the Elliots were not entirely flattering. Mary would probably be the languishing, complaining one, and Anne the faded, unapproachable one.

Miss Elliot was harder. Handsome and proud, certainly. Accomplished or enjoyable... perhaps?

Caroline was almost relieved when Lizzy and Jane arrived, which annoyed her.

Lizzy was glad to be free of Mr. Collins for the afternoon, for she very much dreaded the coming confrontation. Not *one* of her warnings to him had been heeded. A stupid man!

She'd thought of trying to encourage him to dangle after her sister Mary, but even Mary—who moralized more than any girl of eighteen had a right to—didn't deserve to be saddled with him.

Lizzy found herself chatting with Miss Mary Elliot, who seemed to only open her eyes at intervals.

Lizzy began to enjoy testing what would make Mary perk up. "Do you miss Kellynch?"

To this, she got merely a languid hand tilt. "It is dreary in the winter; I am happy to be elsewhere. I'd prefer London, however."

So, this sister was not obsessed with *The Baronetage*.

"Are you usually unwell in the winter?" Lizzy asked. "You look as if you might have a delicate constitution."

Mary sat up abruptly. "Yes, and it is the most *provoking* thing. For Elizabeth will only say that I might be well if I chose, and that *she* feels perfectly fine!"

Lizzy smiled. Mary reminded her more than a little of her mother. "Is it your nerves?"

"Well, not *precisely*, but even if it *was*, it would be odious of Elizabeth to say that I am too young for them! As if nerves only grow as you get older."

"That would be a strange feat of biology, certainly."

"Yes. But for me it is often these terrible colds, and a fatigue that makes my body ache miserably. No one will come near me for days except Anne."

"Ah, is she the caretaker in your family?"

Mary wrinkled her nose. "I suppose, though Anne is almost worse, for she *always* recommends that I should feel better with some exertion. If I am in bed, she wants me out of it. If I am in my dressing gown, she wants me dressed. If I am sitting in the drawing room, she wants me to walk."

"How unreasonable."

"She says it is all for my good, and that I will feel more cheerful after, but she is wrong. To be fair, she does bring me soup and build my fire and read to me for hours, but still. Perhaps to be up and doing makes *her* more cheerful, but how can she know how I feel?"

"'Each heart knows its own bitterness, and no one can share its joy,'" Lizzy quoted.

Mary furrowed her brow. "Is that Shakespeare?"

"A proverb, I think. My father likes to quote it."

"I don't care for proverbs; they're so *smug*."

They were interrupted by the arrival of Mr. Darcy.

Both Caroline and Miss Elliot moved slightly to make space for him. Caroline scooted to the left on the claw-footed divan; Miss Elliot languidly made space on the floral settee.

Lizzy grinned. Miss Bingley and Miss Elliot were very well-matched as competitors. They were both tall, with high color, immaculate curled blonde hair, and even similar bone structure. She watched Mr. Darcy as well, and though his stoic face gave little away, he looked rather as if he regretted entering the room.

He bowed and greeted the guests, took up a newspaper, and sat in one of the Queen Anne chairs near the fireplace.

When the room had settled from his intrusion and Mary had truly fallen asleep, he looked over his paper to Lizzy. "I apologize for my words at the assembly; I ought to have kept my thoughts to myself."

This was not an apology of merit, but Lizzy liked him too little to care. She was merely relieved that he no longer thought her on the catch for him. "Noted, thank you, sir."

She didn't want to dwell on his rudeness, and she was of too lively a temperament to sit here in silence while Mary slept. "You seem to gravitate towards fireplaces, Mr. Darcy. Are you often cold?"

He returned his eyes to his paper. "No."

"And I see that is the same paper you were reading at my house only yesterday. Is it still so interesting?"

He hesitated. "I've not yet finished this article on the proposed Corn Laws."

"My father says the tariffs on foreign grain will help large farmers here in England, but they will drive costs up in the meantime. I think perhaps a graduated introduction of tariffs would help ease the process."

Darcy stared at her. "You have opinions on the grain tariffs?"

"Yes, but I forgot you have not yet finished the article. It is rude of me to discuss it when you can't have formed an opinion yet."

He folded the paper. "Of course I have formed an opinion; this is hardly the first time it's been proposed. It will drive up costs in the short term, but they'll never get approval before the war is done. The Whigs and Tories will argue for at least a few more years before we see the tariffs levied."

"You are severe upon Parliament."

Darcy shrugged. "They do a job I would rather not do, but they do it worse than I would. My gratitude is limited."

"You are confident in your abilities."

"I am a proud man; I don't deny it. But where there is real superiority of mind, pride will always be under good regulation."

"Are you *certain* of that?"

Sir Walter Elliot was even then checking his reflection in one of the mirrors. "Anne has let herself go terribly," he said, "and even our friend Lady Russel shows her age ill. I do not at all understand the problem." He smoothed his hands over his torso. "It is not so hard to maintain a trim figure, yet I see so many men nearly as wide as they are tall, fit to rival the Prince Regent."

Mr. Darcy almost smiled, and it almost improved his face. "A contrary example that still proves my point," he said quietly.

He had leaned toward her, so as not to be overheard, and she had leaned forward to hear.

This could not be borne by some ladies of the household. Lizzy grinned when Caroline joined them.

"Ugh, it is far too hot by the fire, Mr. Darcy. You will be scorched! Miss Lizzy will not mind changing places with you, for her dress is so thin."

"Certainly," Lizzy said, abandoning him to the hunt, "I was just noting that he need not sit by the fire. In fact, you are looking rather flushed, sir, you ought to go to the other side of the room. It is much cooler by the windows ."

Darcy allowed himself to be moved away from Lizzy, as he'd already shown her more attention than he meant to. She took up the newspaper with great aplomb.

He was insensibly glad that she had not taken his harsh words to heart. When she had repeated "barely tolerable" at Longbourn, he had felt an unfamiliar mortification.

He prided himself on his behavior being always above reproach, and in fairness to himself, it generally was. Lizzy must realize that he had not yet met her when he said that, and that he was frustrated with his friend. It really was not an insult to her at all, but rather to his ill mood that evening. It ought not have been overheard, however, and he ought to have made sure it was not.

He would take a lesson from that.

He did not have long to ponder it before Miss Elliot turned to him. "Mr. Darcy, surely *you* understand the onerous nature of tenants who take advantage of the estate? My sister Anne, and even our friend Lady Russel, would have my poor father answering every request with money. Not even a loan, but a gift! As if my father has no other need for funds. It is driving him quite distracted."

Mr. Darcy frowned. "There are certainly tenants who would take advantage of a manager or owner. That's why I employ an excellent steward at Pemberley; otherwise, I should be quite tied there. The master of an estate is responsible for certain upkeep, however."

Sir Walter moved away from the mirror, but then stepped back to smooth his hair. "But stewards, my good man, stewards are thieves as well! They demand an *exorbitant* salary, even in the winter when they cannot be supervising the tenant farms."

"Winter work is vital. They handle repairs on the cottages and barns, help the men bargain for seed, lay in supplies...arguably, the days are shorter, but the work is longer," Darcy said.

Miss Elliot rearranged her wrap. "I don't know about that, but I shall certainly hold an excellent Open Day for our people at Christmas. We always do baskets and gifts for them; Anne arranges it all. *Very* generous."

Mr. Darcy felt his lip curl.

Caroline clasped her hands before he could respond. "Luncheon?"

LIZZY EYED MR. COLLINS WITH DISTASTE and helplessness. He had made her a proposal of marriage, *if* it could be called such when he assumed every answer was yes in hidden form.

"I'm not being feminine or trifling with you, sir," Lizzy repeated. "I am telling you plainly that we should not suit, and I must decline your offer."

He smiled and even patted her hand. "I am quite willing to play the game however long you deem necessary."

"It would be the *height* of folly to make a game of my future, and it would be cruel to make a game of yours."

"I absolve you of cruelty, for I know women must have their little ways."

"That is not what I'm doing! You will need to look elsewhere for a wife."

"I think perhaps this interview has gone as far as it can at present. I will look forward to accompanying you to your aunt's house this evening."

Lizzy fled the room and, after grabbing a bonnet from the hooks in the hall, left the house. If she did not walk off some of her exasperation, she could not answer for the consequences.

She tied the ribbons under her ear with shaking fingers, not from fright or awkwardness but sheer vexation.

Her mother would be unbearable about her refusal. Her father... he would support her, would he not? She felt persuaded he would, but he would do it in some off-hand, laconic fashion which would in no way reconcile or silence her mother.

Lizzy sniffed. The wind was blowing, but it was not so cold and severe as yesterday. This was the lovely part of November, when the last red leaves clinging to the trees were falling one at a time, instead of in torrents. The fallen leaves along the edge of the road were dry and crackly. They crunched as she walked, though her boots squelched in the wet layer underneath.

She headed for Lucas Lodge, but then changed her mind. She could not talk to Charlotte just now. Lizzy headed instead for the road to Meryton. She would not go all the way, but perhaps to the footbridge that crossed the stream.

Of course, it was someone far worse who interrupted her walk: Mr. Darcy, riding his big roan horse.

He was not satisfied with a nod but dismounted to walk next to her.

"Yes?" Lizzy asked. "What is it?"

He looked a little taken aback by her abruptness. "Nothing in particular. Did you see today's article about the grain tariffs?"

"No. My morning was occupied, unfortunately."

He started to tell her something, and his pedantic tone was more than she could take. Perhaps he was not as condescending as all that, but she could not tolerate any more arrogant men this morning.

"I've had a trying morning," Lizzy interrupted, "so I do apologize, but I must not keep you. I'm in no frame of mind to talk politics."

"Ah. Of course." He walked quietly for a moment. "You don't wish to talk to anyone, yet you are headed to town?"

Lizzy threw up a hand. "Yes, you have caught me in an irrational moment. I have provided you an excellent subpoint for future arguments on women's illogic."

Darcy could not mistake this bitter statement for mere liveliness. Lizzy was upset, though he did not flatter himself it had to do with him.

He considered what he'd seen of her family in the last week.

"Has the parson proposed?" he asked.

Lizzy gaped at him. "It is—rude—to allude to a possible private encounter."

He grimaced. "Is it? If you accepted him, it would become known regardless."

"It is also... annoying of you to guess correctly at once. It is far easier to be surrounded by stupid people."

"As you generally are."

Lizzy gasped. "Now you have insulted my family and friends thoroughly, in only four words. I congratulate you."

"I was merely reiterating what *you* said, not insulting your community. Most people cannot help their lack of intelligence. You did say it first."

"I was speaking theoretically. Your pride misleads you. My father is an extremely intelligent man, and though my sister Jane is no show-off, she has an excellent understanding. My friend Charlotte is eminently practical, but she hides a very sound mind."

Darcy was not instinctively good at reading people, but even he knew when to retreat. He didn't think terribly highly of Lizzy's father—the behavior of his wife and daughters, without refinement or even common sense and manners—did not speak well of his abilities. Pure intelligence was not nearly as important as application, in Darcy's opinion, but he suspected he shouldn't bring that up just now.

"I did not mean to cast aspersions on them," Darcy said.

Lizzy took a sharp breath. "Then I apologize for speaking harshly. I ought not to have allowed my frustration to make me react so, even under provocation."

"Perhaps I ought to remove myself and offer no more provocation."

"That would be best."

Darcy remounted his horse. A sudden thought made him hold the reins tight. He'd assumed her ill-humor sprang from the annoyance of having to refuse the annoying Mr. Collins, but she had not specified. Was it possible she accepted him? The thought was intolerable. "You did refuse him, didn't you? The fussy parson?"

Lizzy had regained her self-control. "It is hardly your business."

She was entirely correct. How irritating.

"Forgive me, good day."

# { 4 }

DARCY HAD TO WAIT FOR THREE DAYS to find out the answer at the ball that Bingley had decided to host.

Darcy stretched his shoulders in his black evening coat. He had not worn this particular one since London the previous season. It did not fit as well as he remembered; he must tell his valet.

He really ought to make an appointment with his tailor in London before he returned to Pemberley. Darcy didn't care overly about clothes, but it was bad *ton* to ignore one's duty, even sartorially.

Yet another reason to go to London. He really must run up there soon, and perhaps take Charles with him. Charles's infatuation with Jane Bennet was becoming a trifle concerning.

As soon as they were rid of the Elliots as house guests, he would suggest a visit.

Caroline was still busy greeting the guests as they arrived at the top of the stairs, and though the ball was not formal enough for a butler to announce the guests, Darcy figured he would learn soon if Elizabeth was engaged to Mr. Collins. He would not even have to *ask* in this hotbed of gossip.

If she had accepted him, what then? Why, nothing, except that Darcy would be slightly more disappointed in the world, and in the way fine things tended to be squandered.

The eldest Miss Elliot placed herself next to him; she was dressed in a rather dashing gown of deep green. It was a color he liked; a shame it was wasted on a vapid, vain woman. She was not as vain as her father but arguably worse since he rated her intelligence slightly higher. Not much higher.

"Do you entertain often at Pemberley, Mr. Darcy?"

"No."

"I suppose, lacking a hostess, it would be tiresome. You ought to have brought an aunt or sister to support you."

"I value my aunts highly, but there are none I wish to live with." A vision of Lady Catherine in his home sent a cold shiver down his back. "My only sister is not yet sixteen."

"Poor girl! I lost my own mother at a young age, and it is no easy thing. Anne says our mother's death was hardest on Mary, who is the youngest, but I think Mary was merely seeking attention, as she always does. Thankfully, my dear father is everything to me."

"Quite."

The Bennets arrived along with Mr. Collins. Mr. Darcy frowned. Surely if the man had been rejected, he would have left?

Darcy excused himself from Miss Elliot and, in a move that was utterly beneath him, said good evening to Lady Lucas, the bosom bow of Mrs. Bennet.

"Oh, good evening, Mr. Darcy! Yes, a fine evening for your friend's ball. Have you heard our wonderful news?"

"What is that, ma'am?"

"Why, my eldest daughter has just gotten engaged. Charlotte is to marry Mr. Collins, who will inherit the Longbourn estate. I could never have believed it; such good fortune. In the meantime, she will live in Huns-ford near your own aunt, I believe, Lady Catherine de Bourgh. Mr. Collins has been telling us *much* of her grand estate."

Darcy intercepted a sharp glare from Mrs. Bennet toward Lady Lucas, as she overheard this less than tactful explanation.

Their friendship was clearly on the rocks, and no wonder.

The man had proposed to Lizzy on Wednesday, then turned around and proposed to the Lucas girl? Darcy felt insensibly cheerful, if bemused. Lady Lucas, taking it as a great compliment that the severe Mr. Darcy had unbent enough to congratulate her with real warmth, felt her cup of satisfaction run over.

Lizzy could only wish the ball would end as soon as possible.

Many were congratulating Charlotte on her engagement, and Charlotte accepted it with smiling thanks. Only once did her eyes meet Lizzy's, and a shadow crossed Charlotte's face. Then she turned back to Mrs. Phillips.

Lizzy had not reacted as she ought. She had first disbelieved Charlotte, then strenuously urged her to reconsider. He was such a pompous, stupid little man. The idea of Charlotte with her sly humor, keen mind, and kind heart stuck with him forever was disgusting.

Lizzy ought to have kept it to herself. Charlotte had been vulnerable, and Lizzy had hurt her. Now Charlotte could not be natural with her.

Lizzy drank more deeply of the warm punch than she generally did. It was less sweet than Lady Lucas's, with more lemon, and she liked it very much. It was the only good thing about the evening, barring Bingley and Jane.

Lydia was loud and wild, flirting in an obvious and immature way with the officers. She frequently called to her friends across the room to settle imagined disputes. These gave her the excuse to push on an officer's shoulder or slap his hand.

Lizzy's mother was still angry about losing Mr. Collins, but she was now hovering nearby talking industriously about Jane's soon-to-be union with Mr. Bingley. It was not only a source of joy, but a way to save face.

Lizzy's middle sister Mary had not done anything embarrassing lately, but she was eyeing the pianoforte possessively.

When her Aunt Phillips cornered her, Lizzy nearly turned away. Her aunt looked arch and coy, and her cheeks were flushed a violent red. "You needn't be sly with me, my dear. I don't blame you for turning down Mr. Collins, and so I have told your mother. I hear *Mr. Darcy* is a favorite of yours."

Lizzy physically recoiled. "He is not. I have less than no expectations for him. Why, I told you myself how he insulted me when we first met."

"Yes, you had us all in stitches, but I had it from young Mr. Lucas that Mr. Darcy speaks only to you when he visits Longbourn! And young Miss Mary tells me you spoke for near half an hour about the *corn laws* of all things."

"Mary grossly exaggerates."

"But you *did* speak of politics? What a strange man! I do not blame you for finding that tiresome—what a stupid thing to discuss with a woman!—but I wouldn't throw him over for all that. He is worth far more than Bingley. If he has a preference for you—"

"There is no preference," Lizzy said. "And if there were, I would not want it."

Her aunt shrugged, "Well, I don't want to get your hopes up, but don't be stupid, Lizzy." She went on toward the ham and helped herself to several juicy slices.

Mr. Darcy was currently talking to Lady Lucas, which was odd and unnatural, but he seemed to notice when she looked at him. Lizzy looked away.

She did her best to muddle through the evening. That included searching for, and then *finding* a giggling Lydia in an alcove between the Netherfield ballroom and the room Caroline had designated for cloaks and hats. The alcove probably once held a table or chest, but Miss Bingley had not filled it yet, and Lydia had.

One of the young officers had rested a hand on her waist, and he was enthusiastically stealing a kiss.

Lizzy cleared her throat loudly, and they both jumped. The officer blushed and bowed. "E-excuse me." He beat a hasty retreat.

"Lydia! He was kissing you, and his hand was—"

Lydia tossed her head with a giggle. Her cheeks were a pink. "Don't moralize, Lizzy! It's not like you've never allowed a boy to steal a kiss."

"In fact, I haven't. And that officer wasn't a *boy*."

"Well, I daresay you flay them with your words, and no one has tried. Even *Jane* has kissed a boy!"

"That was young Marcus, barely more than fourteen, and he surprised her in the orchard."

"Well, if I was her, I would have enjoyed it."

Lizzy shook her head. "I don't expect you to hate affection, but Lydia—these officers are not boys. They might want more. You probably don't realize—"

"You think me a baby! Of course I realize what they want. I can take care of myself." Lydia stomped back to the ballroom, and Lizzy let her go.

Their father did not take Lydia seriously as a young lady, so why would Lydia take herself seriously?

While she was still in the corridor, Lizzy heard Anne and Mary Elliot arguing just around the corner. A candle beyond them put their shadows on the wall in front of Lizzy.

Anne Elliot's voice was low and reserved. "Mary, I am sorry you are disappointed that Lieutenant Wickham is not here, but you must not sulk all evening. There are so many other pleasant gentlemen with whom you might dance."

"You are ridiculous to accuse *me* of sulking," Mary said, in an undeniably pettish tone. "You never push yourself to enjoy balls. Why should I? And Wickham *said* he would be here. It is most provoking. It is all Darcy's fault, I'm sure of it."

"You ought not use his name in such a familiar way. Mr. Darcy has been an unexceptional  host to us, along with Mr. and Miss Bingley, of course. You shouldn't believe everything you hear."

Mary tossed her head. "I know suffering when I hear it, and Wickham has certainly suffered at Mr. Darcy's hands. It was the *greatest* injustice. If Wickham had the place he ought to have, he would be an eligible man. Father would at least consider him as a—as—"

"Oh, Mary." Anne's shadow put an arm around her sister's shoulders. "If you truly prefer this Mr. Wickham, time will prove his worth. I will support you with whoever you choose."

Mary shrugged her off. "You are so strange, Anne. As if *your* support would do anything. Nor would I marry a poor man! How stupid."

"If you loved a poor man, but he had gainful employment—not that I am at all sure about Mr. Wickham— I would not counsel you to refuse on *that* score. You will have some portion from Mother as well."

Mary shook out her wrap, and it looked as though Anne helped her re-drape it over herself.

"It's fine," Mary said. "I don't know why I should expect sympathy from you. I just wanted to have a fun night, and instead I get *this*." Mary waved a hand around dismissively as they moved away. Light poured into the hall as they opened the door to the ballroom and reentered.

Despite her non-enjoyment of the evening, Lizzy couldn't help being curious about this story. Mr. Wickham and Darcy? She had observed a rather shocking reaction in Mr. Darcy to Mr. Wickham's presence in town. Unfortunately, she had no one to ask. She'd exchanged no more than nods with Mr. Wickham since that first evening at her aunt's house, and she couldn't approach him with this. She *was* acquainted with Mr. Darcy, more's the pity, but she doubted he would answer. He already though her impertinent and ill-behaved.

Now she was even more intrigued. She collected herself just outside the ballroom door, but the door opened again before she was ready.

It was one of the gentlemen, silhouetted by the brilliant chandeliers behind him. It was Mr. Darcy.

Lizzy dipped her head in acknowledgement. "Excuse me, I was just coming back in."

Mr. Darcy froze in front of the door. He glanced at the alcove a few steps beyond her, as if suspecting she might have been dallying there. In fact, if anyone came upon them in the dark hall, they would assume so.

"Mr. Darcy?" Lizzy lifted her chin. "May I pass?"

"Oh, excuse me." He stepped to the side and held the door for her, even more stiffly than usual.

Darcy followed her back into the ballroom. He'd meant to do something—fetch something?—but he'd forgotten what it was. His memory lapse had something to do with how pretty Elizabeth looked in the low light of the hallway. He'd been quite struck.

"I hear the Reverend Mr. Collins is engaged." Darcy did not precisely mean to speak of the engagement or their previous conversation, but his evil genius prompted him to speak to her since he had the chance, and he said the first thing to come to mind.

Lizzy's eyes grew wide. She still faced the dancers but slanted her head toward him a trifle. "Do *not*, I beg you, say anything to indicate what you guessed last week. It would mortify Charlotte if it were generally known."

"I would never gossip about you or your friend. Or anything for that matter, I despise gossip."

"Yes, yes, you are better than me; I will admit anything you like, only be discreet."

"I'm always discreet."

Her concern gave way to a smile. "I suppose you *are* the last person in the world who needs a warning to say *less*, even if you do not care what your words would do to any of us."

"You are still rather harsh, are you not? I have apologized for my earlier remark."

"You apologized for *my* hearing it, not for *you* saying it."

There was a long silence as he thought back. "I stand corrected. I ought not to have said it."

"Thank you, Mr. Darcy. I appreciate your apology and your discretion."

He felt the urge to prolong the conversation, but Mr. Bingley called to him, and Darcy moved reluctantly away.

Lizzy checked that Lydia was still in the ballroom—drinking negus, thankfully—but then she realized that the rather onerous piano music currently filling the lull in the party was from her sister Mary.

Mary had begun a long concerto that was really beyond her skills. She tended to play it slowly so as to get every note, and that made it even more difficult to listen to. Lizzy moved to one of the sofas near the piano. Perhaps she might encourage Mary to give her seat to another young lady when she was finished.

Bingley came and sat next to Jane, who smiled, but continued her conversation with Miss Elliot. Darcy hovered outside the seating circle.

Miss Bingley patted the sofa next to herself. "Mr. Darcy, will you not sit? You have been out all day and no doubt could use a rest."

"Yes, please do sit," Miss Elliot said. She moved graciously to one side of the love seat as they reprised their competition from Lizzy's last visit. She wondered how often such things went on, with both Miss Bingley and Miss Elliot living at Netherfield with Mr. Darcy.

Miss Bingley gestured to a chair on her other side. "Or sit here, if you would prefer to be a little further from the pianoforte."

Mr. Darcy did not move to sit in either location. "There are a number of available seats, please don't feel the need to enumerate each of them or you will both miss enjoying the—performance."

Lizzy smiled. She hadn't liked Mr. Darcy at first, but there was no denying he was a bold man. He might even hide a sense of humor under that proud exterior. It was no wonder he was a little standoffish if every woman behaved like Miss Bingley and Miss Elliot.

After a moment, when the ladies had turned back to Mary's unending performance and begun to gossip between themselves; Darcy sat on the sofa next to Lizzy.

She only just refrained from laughing. The one woman in the room who did *not* particularly want his company was the one he chose to grace with his presence. Perhaps that was why; he was no doubt tired of women on the catch for him.

He did not speak to her, but he did lean back and extend his legs, crossing his feet as he relaxed.

Bingley sat with Jane, whispering something to her, and they were both oblivious to Mary's weak voice now accompanying her playing.

Mr. Collins sat with Charlotte nearby, speaking of Lady Catherine's divine taste in music. Lydia stood with one of the officers at the other end of the room, flirting, and even Kitty was nearby with the oldest Lucas boy.

Everyone was pairing up and meanwhile she and Mr. Darcy...

With a jolt of unease, Lizzy realized she might have been as blind as Jane. Perhaps Mr. Darcy *did* prefer her. That first insult aside, he had made a point of speaking with her. Perhaps his long, stoic looks, his hovering and listening, were signs of interest?

She glanced at him dubiously, still more than half sure she was wrong.

He shifted as Mary failed to hit a high note, achieving a painful dissonance. He glanced at Lizzy. A smile tugged up one part of his mouth before he seemed to recollect himself. His face smoothed and he looked back toward the piano.

Good *heavens.*

# { 5 }

CAROLINE BINGLEY APPROACHED Mr. Darcy when he was in the breakfast room the following morning.

The remains of beef and eggs were on his plate, and he was nursing a cup of dark tea while reading the new *London Gazette.*

Miss Bingley served herself a muffin and a thin slice of beef from the sideboard. The Elliots were not up yet, except for Anne, whom Caroline could hear playing the piano in the drawing room at the front of the house.

The weak November sunlight was coming in the eastern windows.

"You're up early after a ball," Mr. Darcy commented, turning a page of *Gazette.*

"I could not sleep soundly after last night. It was disquieting on a number of fronts, and I can't but feel that it was partly my fault."

"Food and wine were excellent; you aren't to blame for the rest. Country people will be country people, no matter how it hurts one's ears."

She shuddered. "If you're referring to Miss Mary Bennet's tone-deaf performance, that is the least of my worries. I have, astoundingly, heard worse in London ballrooms."

"So have I, though usually a trifle shorter."

Caroline laughed. "But you must be serious. I'm talking about Charles. He is utterly *besotted* with Jane Bennet—and they think she will marry him before the end of the year. I *heard* Mrs. Bennet say so."

He folded the paper and set it on the table next to his plate. "I heard her say something to that effect also."

"It would be so simple to take Charles away, if not for my inviting the Elliots to stay." Caroline kept her voice down, in case any of them should be nearby, though generally they kept to their rooms quite late. "That is why I say it is my fault. Otherwise, we could make a trip to London, to divert him."

Darcy grimaced. "I hate anything like artifice, but I cannot deny that such a marriage would do Bingley no good. And I do not think—though you would perhaps judge better than I—that Miss Bennet cares as much as Bingley. *Do* you think it? I watched her last night, but

I fear it is largely her mother's ambition which is the undergirding of her amiability."

Caroline took a sip of tea. "I think she genuinely likes him and would marry him—who would not, in her position?—but I believe you are right that her affection is less particular than his. Certainly less effusive."

This was not a lie, Caroline told herself, for very few people had such lively affections as her brother. Caroline suspected that Jane *did* feel more than she showed, but it was not Caroline's job to ferret it out. It was certainly not *her* job to persuade Mr. Darcy of it, no matter what her intuition might hint at.

Caroline folded that thought away and shook her head decidedly. "I do not know precisely how Jane feels, but it was made abundantly clear how her *mother* feels. I do wish we might preserve Charles from this. A fortnight away and he would find another to admire."

"But the Elliots."

"Yes. If I took Miss Elliot into my confidence, however, I believe she would completely support us. She has an extremely fine sense of what is due a family in marriage."

"*Absolutely* not."

Caroline jolted, spilling a bit of tea over her wrist.

"I apologize for my tone," Mr. Darcy said, "but I already feel we are on the edge of behavior that is beneath us. The only saving grace is that we both care deeply for your brother. Miss Elliot is an arrogant, empty-headed female who would not know altruism if it slapped her in the face."

Caroline froze for a moment. She was glad to hear that Mr. Darcy did not rank Miss Elliot above herself, for it was clear Miss Elliot would snatch him up in a *heartbeat* with any encouragement. Caroline even agreed that Miss Elliot was proud and perhaps a little lacking in musical or artistic accomplishments. Despite some small deficiencies, however, Miss Elliot was essentially a higher-born version of Caroline.

Miss Elliot was agreeable in company, intelligent, handsome—although a little beyond the first blush of youth—and destined to marry well. She was stylish and confident. In short, everything Caroline wanted to be. They even looked alike. To hear Mr. Darcy speak of Miss Elliot this way was jarring.

He didn't think of *Caroline* that way, did he?

Well, clearly not, for he was still speaking to her of Charles's predicament. Mollified, if not perfectly reassured, Caroline nodded. "I won't say anything to her, then. But I am not perfectly sure how to get rid of them. I cannot very well go to London with Charles and leave them here *alone*."

IN AN UNEXPECTED TURN OF EVENTS, it was Charles who suggested that he ought to run up to London.

Darcy coughed in surprise when Charles announced it around noon, when the rest of the party had gathered in the drawing room. Anne Elliot had ceased playing the pianoforte. She sat quietly near the mirror by the door, and her reflection had almost more color than she did.

"I know none of you will mind if I do not stand on ceremony," Bingley said in his winning way, "for Caroline will keep you comfortably here. I have a few errands to do and an appointment I must not put off. I thought to leave in the morning."

Darcy nodded. "I might go up with you. I need to see my tailor, and I want to look at the townhouse and make sure it is ready for Georgiana's visit."

"You may accompany me," Charles said, "but don't think to keep me for long. I plan to accomplish my work by Thursday at the latest, so that I might come back north on Friday or Saturday."

Caroline shook her head. "No, Charles, you must not *rush* Mr. Darcy. One should never rush their tailor, should they? I'm sure Sir Walter understands."

"I agree completely!" Sir Walter said.

Mr. Darcy did not like subterfuge, but even he could admit Caroline's superior skill.

"Do you know," added Sir Walter, opening a very fine snuff box which smelt of tobacco and a little mint, "I think I shall take the girls to London. You mention your tailor, Mr. Darcy, and the truth is that I have not gotten a new rig in nearly a twelvemonth."

"It was in the summer, Father," Anne put in.

"The summer? No, I do not think you can be right. Last fall, at the earliest. Possibly spring."

"I believe it was June."

"Well, it is nearly the end of November, so that is a very long time. My good Jacques will have forgotten me, and I am not finding the fit of my latest boots to be quite right."

"Oh, yes, Father," said Miss Elliot, "let us go to London. You have had quite a good visit with Sir William Lucas—far more than he really ought to *expect* of you—and my friends in London will be thrilled to have me before Christmas, even if it is not the height of the Season. I must make invitations! I can arrange quite a holiday house party for Kellynch while we are in town."

Sir Walter clapped his hands. "A plan! Excellent."

Caroline smiled with relief. She could now offer hospitality with the firm conviction it would be rejected. "I would never stand in the way of your plans, but you are welcome at Netherfield as long as you like, of course. I would never wish you to feel rushed or neglected."

Sir Walter tucked his snuffbox away in his coat pocket and went so far as to clasp Caroline's hand briefly. "Not at all, my dear Miss Bingley! You have been a most excellent hostess, and I shall have good things to say about Netherfield and my time here."

"Thank you very much, Sir Walter."

Mr. Darcy allowed himself a moment of relief as well. He didn't fancy living in the same house as Miss Elliot any longer.

"Well, I don't want to go to London just now," Mary Elliot complained. "*Not* that anyone has asked *me*. I have made friends here, and I like it. I want to stay."

"You cannot stay without us," Miss Elliot said.

"You would miss us, surely," Anne added.

"I don't know why I can't stay here with Miss Bingley. Or with the Lucases or the Phillipses. I have finally made some friends, and I won't be parted from them! It is too unkind."

Darcy looked to Caroline. Her plans were being un-raveled.

"That would be a pity," Caroline said, perforce. "Of course, you can stay here."

"I would just as soon stay with the Lucases," Mary said. "They entertain officers three times a week."

Sir Walter shook his head. "The officers are mostly plain, bracket-faced men. What do they look for in re-cruits these days? When I was a young man, the militias were something worth seeing."

Anne frowned deeply. "You have only been out a year, Mary. If you care deeply for an officer—"

"I did not say that, did I? I merely want to have *fun*, which you would not understand, Anne. You stopped having fun before you turned twenty."

This pleasant family spat might have continued indefinitely, but to Darcy's relief, Sir Walter was an indulgent parent.

"I'll ask Lady Lucas," he said. "She would be honored to have you, and we will send for you when we are ready to return to Somerset."

"Father," Anne said. "I truly don't think we ought to leave Mary in an unknown neighborhood alone and unprotected—"

"Hardly unknown," Miss Elliot drawled.

"Nor would I be alone," Mary said.

"Then let me stay also," Anne said. "I would like to stay at the Lucases with Mary."

Sir Walter waved a hand. "Certainly, though I would say, Anne, that *you* need clothes more than the rest of us. I think it's been two years since you ordered something nice. You seem to forget that *we* must look at you."

With such light-handed insults, complaints, and flattery, it was all settled to everyone's satisfaction that the house party would break apart the following afternoon. Anne and Mary to the Lucases, whose compliance with the plan was now assumed. Sir Walter and Miss

Elliot would retire to their town house in London, and Darcy, Bingley, and Caroline to theirs.

Darcy felt a pang at not seeing Lizzy again, but it was for the best. What kind of friend would he be if he endangered Charles's future for his own selfish dalliance? For it was selfish. It made no sense at all to consider a girl in the Bennet family for marriage, so Darcy's growing thoughts of her were even more absurd.

MR. COLLINS'S SHORT BROWN HAIR ruffled in the wind as they all stood in front of Longbourn, waiting for him to finish his leave-taking speeches.

Lizzy did not know why she had expected that the near-freezing wind would shorten them; she was very wrong.

"And to you, my cousin Lizzy," he said finally, "please know that I bear no ill-will, though I do not know how Lady Catherine will take the news. I will endeavor to convey to her the depth of my gratitude to have found my second self, the queen of my future life, in Miss Lucas. What you meant for ill has been turned to good, therefore no reproaches shall ever pass my lips, and we shall forever be silent on what has passed."

*If only*, Lizzy thought.

He finally got in the carriage and Lizzy and the others waved him off. Her father had already retreated inside the warm house, and Mrs. Bennet quickly followed.

Kitty coughed violently from the entryway, and Jane put her arm around her. "You ought to be in bed, sounding like that! Poor Kitty. I will have Alice brew you a posset so you can rest. You were coughing all night, I think."

Lydia pouted as she came back in. Her cheeks were red from the wind, and her eyes were restless. "I cannot *bear* to be cooped up again in the house! Lizzy, say you will come with me to Meryton. I want to buy new ribbons for that ugly bonnet I bought."

"It is very cold to be walking," Jane said. "You will be as sick as Kitty if you continue."

"I never get sick," Lydia said. "I'm too stout and strong."

"That you are," said Mrs. Bennet, settling into the long sofa with a pillow behind her head and a shawl over her feet, ready for a nap. "The stoutest, prettiest baby I had, except for Jane, and the loudest at crying. Oh, the nurse had the worst time with you," she congratulated her.

Lizzy warmed her hands by the fire. "If the wind dies down this afternoon, I'll walk in with you."

IN MERYTON, WITH THE FALL sunlight breaking through the shifting layers of high clouds, and the wind dying down enough that it barely scudded the leaves along the cobblestones, Lydia and Lizzy visited their favorite milliner.

Lydia came away with new ribbons of white, yellow, and pink, and Lizzy came away with the uncertain news that most of the Netherfield party had left for London.

Jane had had no warning of this. Hopefully Mr. Bingley would be back soon, but it was odd.

Several officers were in the street as she and Lydia walked back through Meryton, and they fell into step beside them. Captain Denny was a friend of Lizzy's, and he walked with her, while the new Lieutenant Wickham walked behind with Lydia.

"Do you think your militia will be stationed here all winter?" Lizzy asked. "Your men seem quite settled in."

"It delights the Home Office to move a militia just when it makes *least* sense, so I cannot promise that we will be here all winter. We rarely land in such good society."

"And is Mr. Wickham fitting in well?"

"Oh, yes. A little more popular with the ladies than with his fellow officers, perhaps, but he seems a good sort."

"Seems? You don't know him?" Lizzy glanced back at them. Lydia was trailing her hand down Wickham's red sleeve.

"I met him when he joined a few months ago. I believe he's from somewhere up north. Cheshire? Lincolnshire?"

"Derbyshire?" Lizzy suggested.

"Yes! That was it. You can see I have not achieved captain on the strength of my memory. I need a wife for that sort of thing."

"I believe he was acquainted with Mr. Darcy, the gentlemen staying at Netherfield."

"Was he? Didn't know that."

Denny clearly knew nothing of their history, and Lizzy felt a little silly for pushing.

Soon they bid adieu to Wickham and Denny, though she and Lydia were not long alone, for they came across Mrs. Long. She was another neighbor, very worthy though a bit gossipy. She sat in her low, open carriage with a stranger driving her.

*He* was a solid, good-looking young man, with a quantity of curly brown hair and a rather large chin.

"Hallo, Miss Lizzy, Miss Lydia!" Mrs. Long called. The man pulled up with a friendly smile.

"What do you know?" Mrs. Long continued. "I have my cousin's son visiting this week! I didn't tell you, for

Corrie Garrett

I didn't know, but a pleasant surprise it is. May I present Mr. Charles Musgrove?"

# { 6 }

ANNE ELLIOT WAS STARTLED BUT PLEASED to see Charles Musgrove enter the Lucas drawing room that evening.

She and Mary had gotten settled back at Lucas Lodge only that day. The Lucases were very gracious at the lack of notice, but Anne fully felt the rudeness of her family's abrupt departure and return.

As gracious as the Lucases were, however, their house was overwhelming.

Currently their parlor, where there were no less than *six* Lucas children, also held Sir William and Lady Lucas, the Bennets—excepting Mrs. Bennet and Kitty, who were not feeling well—and now Mr. and Mrs. Long. It was loud, bright, and chaotic. There were also at least six officers present, and Anne felt the oncoming of a headache.

*Starch and Strategy*

Two of the youths had begun a game of lottery tickets, which was a lively game with unpredictable shrieks of victory. Lydia and Mary were teasing the Lucases' cat, which meowed loudly above the general clink of teacups, saucers, and spoons.

Anne's sister Mary had now moved near an ingenious rocking horse, where she was talking to Lieutenant Wickham. Mary pushed on the horse's wooly head and laughed as Wickham made the reins dance in approximation of a cavalry trick. Anne knew she could not prevent Mary talking to Mr. Wickham, but she tried to keep an eye on them.

For the first time, Anne understood how young she must have looked to Lady Russel when Captain Wentworth first appeared. She must have looked just as young as Mary now did to her—and they had gotten engaged so quickly. He hadn't even been *Captain* Wentworth then, only a lowly midshipman with dreams.

Even though she had been young when he proposed, Anne had long since decided she was wrong to doubt herself. It had been a mistake to break her engagement to him, and every year that passed made her realize that it was not one she could rectify. Perhaps if she had something else to invest her mind and energies and heart into, she might have been able to forget. Alas, she did not. Someday when her sisters married she might enjoy their children—but even that did not convey much joy. Anne liked children, but she couldn't fool herself that being a caretaker was her highest ambition.

Anne was suspicious of Mr. Wickham, but she would not blight Mary's chance for love if he proved sincere.

Her quiet observance was interrupted when she realized that Charles Musgrove, a dear friend from her home, had entered with the Long family.

"What? Charles?" She'd known him since they were children, and she rose happily at the sight of his familiar face, temporarily forgetting that warmer considerations had lately constrained her in his presence.

She held out her hands, and he gripped them in his solid way. His fingers were rectangular, rather like his face and mind.

"Well met, Anne! How do you do?"

"Better, for seeing you. I need all the news from Uppercross."

"And you shall have it. Hullo, Mary," he said.

Mary paused in her conversation with Wickham. "What are you doing here?" she laughed. "Did you miss us? Let me introduce my friend, Lieutenant Wickham."

Introductions were made with Wickham and the other members of the party, but eventually Mr. Musgrove came back to sit with Anne.

His smile was as sturdy as ever, but there was a tender light in his eyes that made Anne recall the past six months. She gently withdrew her hand from his and sat on a wooden chair that would put him at a slight distance.

If he noted her withdrawal, he did not show it, and he usually showed everything on his face.

"Lady Russel sends her love," Charles started. "And bids me to make sure that you are not being neglected by your family."

Anne smiled. "I never am neglected; merely, occasionally, ignored."

"Hm. My sisters send their love as well," he said. "Henrietta wishes you to visit in December, so that she might show you all she has learned at school since the summer. My mother seconded it, by the way."

"And what of your brother Richard? Has he been assigned a ship yet?" Anne could not help her avid interest in all things related to the British navy.

"Not that we have heard, but it cannot come too soon. He got involved in a gaming hell in Brighton to the tune of five hundred pounds." Charles shook his head. "I fear he is as wild as ever. Who else would even *find* a gaming hell in Brighton? Such a sapskull."

"Hopefully the rigors of the sea will settle him."

"Hopefully." He told her more of their mutual friends, of the rector getting a curate to help while he was unwell, and of one of his tenants who lost part of a barn due to flooding.

"I got all that settled before I came away," he added.

"I was sure of it." Charles was a responsible man, and a benefit to his father. He would inherit one of the largest parcels of land in the district eventually.

"Anne..." He lowered his voice. "You didn't let me ask a question when I last saw you in Uppercross."

Anne winced. "I'm sorry."

"I wouldn't have chosen to say this in company, but I don't know when I'll have another quiet moment with you." He took a deep breath. "Will you not marry me, Anne? I know you would have let me speak sooner, if the answer was yes, but I have to ask. We would be happy, you know. I'm just an average, practical man, but we have been friends for years. I admire you, and my mother likes you. My sisters do, too. And at Uppercross you would not be far from Kellynch. Would you consider it?"

Anne looked sadly at his nervous square face and his tense, sturdy frame. He was a perfectly fine young man, but she did not love him, and she knew what it felt like to love. She had come so close to a marriage of true affection and passion—she could not bring her broken heart to weigh down poor Charles. And she couldn't, quite, relinquish the idea of Frederick Wentworth.

"I can't, Charles. I am sorry. It wouldn't be right, and it wouldn't make either of us happy."

"I think I might be."

Anne smiled. "Well, perhaps you would be happy, but I still cannot."

He sighed. "I suspected you would say that, or else you would not have redirected me at Uppercross. Would you like me to wait and ask again next year?"

"That is kind of you to offer, but no."

"Ah, well. My sisters and my mother will be disappointed."

"Hopefully not for long. You're a great catch for anyone."

Now it was his turn to grimace. "Am I? You know me, Anne. I am practical, and I like best people that I know. The thought of trying to woo some girl I'm barely acquainted with is... nerve-wracking."

Anne smiled. She suspected a large part of his attachment to her was merely proximity and familiarity, but she hadn't realized he was aware of it. "What a terrible task. At least you are not naturally stern and taciturn like one of the men we've stayed with recently. You have only to be your usual self."

"Louisa said that too, only then she went on to list all the things I ought to change about my usual self! I no longer trust women when they say that." He looked around. "I suppose I cannot sit in your pocket all evening. I will take myself off for now."

Charlotte Lucas had not meant to eavesdrop on Anne Elliot and Mr. Musgrove. As soon as she realized what she was hearing, she moved away.

It was enough however, that she felt some pity for the both of them.

Mr. Musgrove soon walked away from Anne, and if his heart was broken, he was too well-bred to display it. He looked a little blindly around the room, and perhaps finding Charlotte the least stressful of the options, came to assist her with the heavy folder that held music for the pianoforte.

Charlotte picked up the messy pile of loose sheet music, left from her younger sisters, and begun to organize it.

"Allow me to lift open the hinge for you, Miss Lucas. Your hands are full." He opened the wooden case that covered the keys, and then set the foldable music stand upright.

Charlotte was able to set the folder down and free up another hand for organizing. "Thank you."

"Not at all." He visibly cast about for something to talk about. "I—er—your mother told me you became engaged last week. Congratulations."

The poor man must have marriage on the mind, after just being rejected.

"Thank you," Charlotte said. "I am very happy."

"Yes." He fiddled with the bent corner of a sheet. "It is a fine thing to be settled."

"Yes." Charlotte was understanding now why he didn't feel confident in wooing a woman he did not know. If he was this uncertain with a woman who was safely engaged, what was he like elsewhere?

Taking pity on him, and thinking how Lizzy would laugh at the conversation, if she and Lizzy were talking right now, Charlotte changed the subject to one where he might shine. "Are you much addicted to sport, Mr. Musgrove? My brother John is home from school and will probably go shooting tomorrow."

"Ah, is that so? I do like to shoot, yes, though I need not intrude on your brother. Does he have success with the game here?"

"He brought back a brace of grouse and a woodcock yesterday."

"That's quite a good haul, particularly as grouse season will end soon."

"That is exactly what John said."

"He must be a good shot. I am tolerable, though I will admit that at times luck has more to do with my success than skill."

"I hear that luck favors the skillful."

"In my experience, luck favors whoever spends *longest* in the field, be he ever so talented or no." He gestured to himself.

Charlotte laughed. "And what do you prefer to shoot? Or do you prefer fox hunting?"

"No, I've done it on occasion, but I'm not so frivolous or finicky as that. Fowl's my preference. I give my game to my mother's cook and enjoy the meals it makes." He thought. "My father does have a trophy room, come to think of it, though we just call it the dark parlor, for it does not get very good light. He has several good deer trophies there, but we're a practical people."

"I can see that. And do you have siblings?"

"Lord, yes. I'm the oldest, but there are seven more after me. My brother Richard just joined the navy as a midshipman, though we hope he'll soon move up. Then there's Henrietta and Louisa, only a year apart and nearly done with school. They'll be out next year, and they're good girls. Then there's four younger ones— but I shan't burden you with their names and ages and expect you to remember them."

Charlotte shook out a music sheet that had been crumpled. "I am the eldest of seven, as perhaps Mrs. Long has told you, so I perfectly understand."

"Exactly. If I marry soon, my youngest brother will be nearly contemporary of my children."

The poor man really *could* not turn his mind far from Anne and marriage.

"For me it would be a larger gap, for my youngest sister is already eleven. I must be several years your senior, but I do understand what you mean."

"Congratulations again on your engagement." He sighed. "It seems strange to me that something so important as one's spouse is left so much to chance and good fortune. We plan our crops beforehand and buy seed in the winter; we plan an addition to the house for *years* in advance. And yet, for marriage, there is *no* plan, *no* guidebook—we are simply meant to do our best."

"It is a sadly mismanaged business, as my friend Lizzy would say. But—excuse me if I overstep, though perhaps being engaged gives me license to speak a little more freely—but you are in an excellent position. You have land and good sense—two powerful inducements to marriage."

"One would think so," he said quietly.

Charlotte felt, rather insensibly, resentful of Anne. Mr. Musgrove, even on the basis of one meeting in town and one evening at her home, was clearly an excellent young man. He was not amazing to look at, but most men weren't. Charlotte was not much moved by men's looks. Even Mr. Darcy and Mr. Bingley, whom everyone had much admired at first, had not caused any flutter in her heart.

Charlotte did not regret accepting Mr. Collins. She was quite satisfied, as a matter of fact, and the relief that she would not grow to be a poor old maid and a burden on her parents was so sharp as to be painful.

She was not stupid, however. She fully recognized that there would be indignity in uniting herself with Mr. Collins. She would never outwardly criticize him, and after she was married, she would endeavor not to *inwardly* either, but if Mr. Musgrove and Mr. Collins were placed in the balance, there could be no comparison.

She already knew Mr. Musgrove to be humble, good-humored, and respectful. How could Anne Elliot simply turn him down?

Anne's father was a baronet, of course, but Anne surely didn't want to be an old maid either? Anne was pretty in a faded way, but she looked older than her years. Still, she *was* prettier than Charlotte, so she would probably receive better offers. Her father was wealthy and titled, and that changed every equation.

Charlotte shook her head as she began to play music so that some of the others might dance. Mr. Musgrove went off to dance with the Elliot sisters, starting with Anne, but then moving to Mary. He also danced with

Jane and Lizzy, though Jane looked rather wan. She must be missing Mr. Bingley.

Lizzy avoided Charlotte's eyes, as per their new normal.

Charlotte played song after song and thought of a snug parsonage in the south that would someday be her domain.


George Wickham looked handsome and noble in his new regimentals for the militia, and he knew it. The Lucases' parlor was a little lacking in grandeur, however.

The curtains were worn, the mortar around the fireplace cracked and peeling, and the sideboard cluttered. The wind occasionally blew a gust of smoke back in, lending an ashy smell to the whole.

Still, Wickham knew he cut a dashing figure among the provincial girls and country gentlemen.

He'd always been good with women, but with the uniform, eligible women were predisposed to trust and admire him. They practically *melted* if he showed attention.

It was amusing, and he was not above taking advantage of it. Hopefully, he could take advantage of it all the way up to a good marriage.

Mr. Darcy had fully cocked up his plan last spring with young Georgiana Darcy. It had been *so* close! That still rankled. Georgiana's fortune would have settled him for life, and it's not as if she wouldn't have been *happy.*

Wickham genuinely liked her, and he would have taken good care of her. It would've been easy, with her fortune.

Darcy's accusations were groundless and bad-tempered. He was jealous of Wickham's popularity with others and with Darcy's father.

The Lucases' house felt all the warmer and more inviting for the knowledge that Darcy would not enter any time soon. Wickham had been a little concerned that Darcy was staying near Meryton, but apparently Darcy had said nothing (false and slanderous) about Wickham.

When the dancing began, Wickham did his part among the young ladies, though he kept a special eye out for Mary Elliot. She was ripe for the plucking, and her father was a wealthy baronet. Wickham was far from certain her father would countenance such a match, but it was worth a push.

She wasn't much to look at—small, with a snub nose—but her figure wasn't bad. As they danced, he evaluated the other women as well, instinctively.

The only one who really caught his eye was Elizabeth Bennet. She was the most interesting of the local women, and had a kissable, impertinent mouth. If he had nothing to satisfy but his own preference, he would have pursued her, at least for a dalliance while the militia was nearby. But with Mary throwing off all sorts of invitations, he would be foolhardy in the extreme to throw away the opportunity.

So it was Mary to whom he'd told his story of ill-usage, of how Darcy had spurned what should have been Wickham's inheritance from his father and a secure position in the church. Mary had been suitably outraged. She shared stories of her own vile mistreatment and neglect at home, encompassing such *heinous* crimes as Anne forgetting to even ask if Mary wanted to pass out holiday baskets to the tenants, and her oldest sister getting more new dresses this summer.

Wickham was chatting with Mary's sister Anne when the topic of Darcy arose again. The Lucases had provided walnuts for roasting, and though Miss Mary was above "such a childish pastime," Wickham was gamely poking the chestnut skin before placing the nut on the stick to roast. He always participated enthusiastically when possible. It was the best way to garner goodwill among hostesses.

Anne was also poking a chestnut with a sharp prong, which would prevent it exploding in messy and dangerous fashion when it grew hot.

"I understand you're acquainted with Mr. Darcy," Anne said.

"Yes, that's right, from our childhood." Wickham was not surprised by this question; he had assumed Mary would tell her sisters his story. He sighed. "I apologize. His name always brings back of host of fond memories of his father, a truly estimable man, but it also brings back many regrets and disappointments."

Lizzy Bennet was supervising her younger sisters at the adjacent table, presumably to make sure they did not impale their fingers while simultaneously flirting with the men around them. Lizzy looked over at them. "If it is not intrusive, what regret connects you and Mr. Darcy, sir? I admit, I am curious."

"It is the most outrageous thing," Mary said on his behalf. "Darcy's father meant for Wickham to have the living near Lambton, where they grew up, but instead, out of jealousy, Darcy *denied* him."

Wickham studied another chestnut sadly. "I cannot blame him too much. It would be trying to know one's father preferred another, and his father was not always tactful about it. I have found a profession, you see; I am determined to neither need nor want anything from the Darcy family again."

The Bennets were now listening as well.

"Stars, that is terrible," Lydia said. "He is just as bad as you thought, Lizzy. Worse!"

"But I thought you were on terms of good friendship with Mr. Darcy and Mr. Bingley," Wickham said.

"Please don't feel you must abuse your friends to assuage *my* feelings. I will never try to vilify the son while his father lives in my memory."

Lydia looked suitably impressed by his generosity, but Anne and Lizzy were a harder audience.

Anne looked troubled, and Lizzy questioned him. "Surely there was a legal recourse, if he denied what his father intended for you."

"It was sadly more informal than that."

"Did he leave many of his affairs unsettled and informal? That sounds irresponsible for a Darcy."

"Oh no, he was much like his son in responsibility, if nothing else. His affairs were in excellent order, though he died untimely of a stroke."

"But others knew of his desire to give you the living?"

"Undoubtedly, but Darcy can be very persuasive. Indeed, I think his jealousy has truly persuaded him that I am altogether contemptible, and that his father was taken in by me. He believes he does right, therefore I cannot hold it entirely against him."

"I would," said Lydia. "He is proud and disagreeable. He probably knew exactly what he was doing."

"I did not find him so," said Anne.

"Proud, yes," said Lizzy, "but not so entirely without a sense of humor as I first thought. He also apologized to me for a rude comment, which I did not expect. If anything, I would've expected his immense pride to *compel* him to honor his father's wishes."

"His pride *has* prompted most of his right action," Wickham agreed, "and among friends he can be very amiable. His unreasoning dislike is limited to me."

"Not entirely to you," Lizzy said. "He found plenty to dislike here, too. Despite that, I would not have suspected him of this sort of injustice."

"I could only wish it were so." Wickham pulled his chestnut from the flames as its shiny brown exterior split open. "But you will never hear me criticize him."

Lizzy laughed. "But what is this conversation if not all of us criticizing him?"

Wickham used a cotton cloth to pull his chestnut off the roasting stick. He allowed a repentant look to cross his face. "I ought to have withheld my history, you are right. Please forgive my indiscretion. Seeing him after so many years brought it all to the surface again."

Lydia and Mary protested that he need not feel bad to tell *them* his story, and that he had *every* right to expose Darcy.

Lizzy and Anne did not add to their reassurance.

IN LONDON, DARCY RESTED HIS HANDS on the back of a blue sofa, while Miss Bingley played the pianoforte for her dinner party guests.

She had already encouraged two other young London misses to play, and now it was her turn to show her superiority at the art.

Mr. Darcy was just returning from the dining room, where the men had lingered to have a glass of brandy after dinner. Bingley filed in after him, along with Sir Walter Elliot, and several other gentlemen Caroline had invited.

The Bingley town house was in Grosvenor Square, bought from a broken-down man-about-town who'd had to sell. The drawing room was navy blue and gold, with cream walls, quite classic. He appreciated that Miss Bingley did not go after every whim of fashion.

Caroline played well, if methodically, and smiled at the gentlemen as they entered. She was a good hostess, and she would probably set up cards or another quiet amusement until teatime.

Miss Elliot came to stand next to him, gently grazing his arm with her bare one. "Good evening, Mr. Darcy. You were seated far too near the end of the table; you haven't said hello to me all evening."

That was not an accident, but Darcy only nodded. "Unfortunate. How do you do, Miss Elliot?"

"Very well. My father and I would love to have you visit us before you return to Hertfordshire. You and Mr. and Miss Bingley, of course. I am having a small gathering on Friday next."

"Thank you. I do not know if I will be able to attend."

"Oh, no! Will you be returning north so soon? Caroline made me think it would be a week or two at least."

"I am not perfectly sure." Darcy reluctantly submitted to the rules that prevented him being as harsh as he wanted. Miss Elliot was a lady and did not deserve his churlishness, however she might behave. "If we are still in town, I will be able to accept your invitation."

"Excellent! Now I have only to work on Mr. Bingley."

Darcy hoped she would succeed in convincing Bingley to stay in London. He had not yet told Bingley his suspicion that Jane was only encouraging him because her mother wanted the match. That idea, if it took root, would keep Bingley in town, but Darcy felt himself strangely loath to do so. Poor Bingley would be quite crushed.

Contrarily, Darcy found himself less enthusiastic about staying in town than he'd expected. He had not reckoned on London with Miss Elliot and her father, and he was now thinking with some fondness of Netherfield without them.

Caroline finished her song, and thankfully, the other young ladies had had their turns. Miss Elliot did not play. The card tables were brought out, and Mr. Darcy almost congratulated himself on an evening done. Then Caroline came and slipped her hand around his elbow. "You will be my partner, will you not, Mr. Darcy? We shall fleece Miss Elliot and her father, I've no doubt!"

Caroline's table, set for four, was ready for him.

"I'm afraid I'm not in the temper for casino or piquet—"

"Of course not, but I know you play whist, and enjoy it. Do not abandon me, please."

Darcy stifled a sigh. Caroline probably deserved a little support from him. "Yes, of course."

He paid penance for his charitable action the rest of the evening, as Miss Bingley and Miss Elliot vied for his attention and admiration.

He wondered if Lizzy played whist. With her, he thought he might prefer chess.


Darcy and Charles sat in the study after Caroline's dinner party was over. Charles loosened his cravat until he could untie it, then tossed it on his desk. He whistled cheerfully and tunelessly as he poured a glass of deep red Madeira for himself and another for Darcy.

"I'm gratified Caroline had a pleasant night," Charles said, "and your cousin Fitzwilliam is always a good time, but I'm glad we can head back to Hertfordshire on Thursday."

He handed one glass to Darcy and sat on the leather chair opposite him, next to the low fire in the grate. The study was a little too opulent, a little too much gilt and too many curlicues, but it had been decorated by Charles's father.

"About that," Darcy began, "I have a few more things to do in town. Can we delay a little?"

Charles rolled the wine in his mouth before swallowing. "We can, of course, or you could post up later on your own. I'd rather not delay long; I told Jane I would be back before Friday." He took another sip. "What's that face, Darcy? Don't tell me you don't like

Jane! She's absolutely unobjectionable, as my mother would have said. An angel, more like."

"I don't *dis*like Miss Bennet, but she is not unobjectionable. Surely you wouldn't want to be saddled with Mrs. Bennet as your mother-in-law for life. Her entire family is an objection."

Charles waved a hand. "Mrs. Bennet is a little tactless and sometimes forward, but she means well. She keeps a good cook and sets an excellent table, you must admit. At least she does not intimidate me, the way the posh London mothers do! You must be used to it more than I, for half the ladies in London would drop their handkerchief for you."

"It's different, Charles. Mrs. Bennet isn't just ambitious, she's... crass. Mr. Bennet is a gentleman, but she is a tradesman's daughter through and through. You can't hide that sort of thing."

"And if I were marrying *her*, perhaps that would weigh with me. You seem to forget that my grandfather was in trade."

"I don't forget anything, but your grandfather doesn't need to live with you."

"Nor would Jane's parents."

"When her father dies, Longbourn will go to Mr. Collins. Where do you think Mrs. Bennet and the other girls will end up? If you are right there at Netherfield, they will land on your doorstep and never leave."

Charles paused with his wine halfway to his mouth, a stricken look on his face.

"Exactly. And the younger girls are vulgar flirts—beyond even what just-fledged girls tend to be."

Charles grimaced and set his wine down. "Point taken. You've made me cringe, as was no doubt your aim. But still, Jane is worth it. We'd get the other girls married off somehow, and we'd set up Mrs. Bennet with—Oh, I know, we'll support her establishment in town with her sister, Mrs. Phillips."

It was not a terrible plan, and under other circumstances, Darcy would have given full credit to Charles for thinking ahead.

Instead he frowned. "Are you sure she is worth it?"

Charles ignored this. "I notice you did not mention Miss Elizabeth."

Darcy tensed. "She is not so problematic or annoying as the others."

"True, she makes me laugh. If she ended up living with Jane and I for some reason, I doubt *you'd* mind overly much." Charles's teasing tone could not be mistaken.

"On the contrary, I'd mind it excessively."

Charles laughed. "Only because you're attracted to her, but you won't admit it."

"I will admit it, but I'd no more attach myself to that family than I'd attach you to it."

"I'm not a sleeve that you get to attach or rip free," Charles said. "I care about Jane. In fact, I love her. I'm going back to Netherfield. You need not come back if seeing Lizzy would give you pain, but you're always welcome there."

Darcy would have to use the trump card; he did not like it. "Do you think Jane cares as much for you as you do for her?"

Charles sank back in his chair, his face flushed from his declaration. "No, probably not. She's had several suitors, I think, probably some of them smarter and better-looking than I. But she likes me quite well, and I am certain she would grow to love me. I mean—dash it all—*you* even like me and you don't like anyone. Surely she would be happy with me."

Darcy felt a surge of regret; he didn't want to crush his friend. "Of course she would be fine, and of course you're an excellent friend. It is only that... having observed her at Netherfield and on other occasions, I didn't see any marked partiality on her part. She is generally pleasing with everyone, down to the serving maids, and I don't want you to be disappointed. I would hate for you to marry her and realize most of her motivation was her mother's urging."

Charles looked down at his hands and swallowed. "I'll allow that my view of her is biased by my wishes. Maybe I've read too much into her complaisance because I want it. But are you certain you're not being swayed by *your* wishes? That she seems indifferent because you want her to be?"

"That's a fair question. I cannot be a hundred percent certain of my judgement, but I truly don't think she's acting like a girl in love, or—er—on her way to it."

"Oh." Charles sat for some time in silence, and Darcy did not interrupt. Eventually, Charles finished his wine. "I'll think on what you've said. Goodnight, Darcy."

CAROLINE SAW DARCY AGAIN at breakfast, since he was staying with them while his town house was refitted.

This time she was the one who had eaten first, and she had lingered over her toast and tea, hoping he would come down.

He looked a bit red around the eyes as if he'd not slept well, and there was a wrinkle between his brows that was not normally there. For a moment she could perfectly picture what he would look like as an older man, in his fifties say, and she wanted that future so much she could hardly speak.

He would be distinguished, wealthy, responsible—still very handsome, of course—and why shouldn't *she* be the one he spent his life with? She understood him, and she would be an excellent mistress of Pemberley.

He helped himself to a few slices of cold ham—men always wanted meat in the morning!—and sat across from her.

"Did you not sleep well?" Caroline asked. "You look a bit hagged."

"No, I didn't. Finally fell asleep a few hours ago."

"I'm so sorry. Is there anything wrong with your guest chamber?"

"The room is fine."

Caroline knew she probably ought to stop pushing him first thing in the morning—no one liked that—but she had so few moments with just him; it was hard to be wise. "Did you speak with Charles?"

"Yes, I did. That's what kept me up."

"How did it go?"

"I told him the truth, but—I don't want to discuss it."

"It's hardly gossip with *me*; I'm his sister."

"I know." He looked out the window toward Grosvenor Square.

Men could be so frustrating. "You're not thinking of letting him go back to Hertfordshire, are you?"

"I'm not his keeper."

"No, of course not, but let's not fool ourselves. Charles listens to everything you say, as well he ought!

You have such good instincts, and he has none." She smiled, but Darcy did not smile back at her.

"I'll be out this morning," Darcy said. "Please let Charles know I'll be back by noon."

Caroline swallowed her last two mouthfuls of cold tea with about the same amount of satisfaction as the conversation had given her.

Darcy went for a walk through the Grosvenor Square garden. The wet lawn darkened the toes of his boots, but they were waxed and waterproof and he didn't feel the chill.

He doffed his beaver-trimmed hat to the few other genteel park patrons he passed, and narrowly dodged a spinning hoop sent rolling across the path by a pair of young boys trailed by their nurse.

It was mid-morning, but the clouds were thick, and London was as gray as a charcoal drawing. The only color was provided by the hardy grass and the deep green of the few pines that had not lost their leaves.

He was not at all sure that he was doing the right thing with Charles, and he hated that feeling. Absolutely upright behavior was his standard for himself, and he accepted nothing less. Generally his feelings confirmed any necessary action.

It was true that the Bennets could destroy the credit and respectability Charles's family had gained in the last ten years. It was also true that Charles was in love with Miss Bennet. His silence last night was most telling, as Charles was never silent.

Once Charles took a fall while they were hunting, and his shoulder had been dislocated. He'd *still* not stopped talking. Charles had cursed a bit at first—understandably—and then been game as a pullet while Darcy and his groom helped him mount the horse and walk back. It must have jarred his shoulder fiercely before they made it to the local doctor in Lambton, but he'd only made jokes about the rough terrain and the story he'd have to tell.

The kind of pain that would make Charles actually *shut up* must be considerable.

The makings of a happy marriage were something of a mystery to Darcy, and he was convinced they were a mystery to everyone, even those who claimed otherwise. In theory, he believed that almost any two people could make a marriage work—it was more of a partnership, after all—but in practice, he found that he didn't want to marry just anyone. Darcy had found, in fact, as he approached the age of twenty-five, that he was quite fussy. Why would he think Charles any less?

Darcy had always been a fastidious boy—disliking mess in his food, clothes, or belongings—and he was apparently just as fastidious in choosing a wife. Miss Elliot was the latest in a lengthy line of acquaintances that made their interest in him—and his twenty thousand pounds a year—very blatant. In looks, she was much like Caroline, but she had more vanity and less intelligence.

Caroline wanted to marry him, and he'd considered her. She wasn't a bad sort, but he had all but decided against her last year.

So why did he get fixated on a country girl whose only real attributes were a quick mind, a slim figure, and beautiful eyes? He was just as shallow as he sometimes accused Charles of being.

Darcy left the park and cut south on Davies Street toward Manton's Shooting Gallery. He needed to purge his misgivings with action.

In the shooting gallery, he was known.

"Ah, Mr. Darcy. You are here to shoot," Manton asked, "or are you looking for a friend?" Joseph Manton was a middle-aged man of large features and rather rough appearance, which somehow the dress of a gentleman didn't quite disguise. Darcy liked him.

"Just here to shoot, please," Darcy said. "I've not brought my own pistol."

"I am happy to furnish Mr. Darcy with a loan. Right this way."

In the gallery there were two other gentlemen present, and one of them, to Darcy's surprise and displeasure, was Sir Walter Elliot. The man never rose before noon at Netherfield, but somehow in London he rose by nine to go shooting?

"Yes, you observe me up at this ungodly hour!" said Sir Walter, after he had introduced Darcy to his friend. "I am up betimes, for my milliner could only fit me in early, and one must occasionally sacrifice to be well-hatted." He laughed at his turn of phrase. "Thankfully I've no need of a perruquier, though you, Grantham, might soon be in need of one." He raised his eyebrows at his friend's receding hair line and thinning red hair.

"Good day, gentlemen." Mr. Darcy moved further down the gallery as he saw that Manton was waiting for him with a pistol. Darcy was not wearing a shooting jacket, as he would in the country, so he merely placed the extra shot and charges on one of the small wooden tables.

Manton set up a wafer for Darcy, a small white disc a little larger than a one-crown coin. He had a basket of them on each table, and often took bets between gentlemen, or even himself, as to how many they could shoot out of twenty.

Darcy didn't particularly want to bet. He just wanted to shoot and stop feeling like a callous heel for crushing his friend's dream.

The first wafer went up in a puff of paste. The next likewise.

It was a double-barrel pistol, so after the second shot he reloaded, wiping his fingers on the cotton cloth provided when he was done.

The next two went up likewise.

Sir Walter sauntered over to join him, his old-fashioned, high-heeled shoes clicking lightly on the wood floor. "A good run so far."

Mr. Darcy shot another. "Thank you, sir."

After six or seven shots, the flint-lock pistol needed to be shaken out, wiped, and fully reloaded with powder.

"My daughter Elizabeth is anxious to stay in town," Sir Walter said. "But I have no great desire to do so. Wish to visit some friends in Bath."

Darcy had no idea why Sir Walter would think he cared. He wiped his hands and shot another wafer.

"Don't like to displease Elizabeth, she's been a good companion since her mother died."

"Then stay," Darcy said.

"She is as handsome as she ever was. She is closer to thirty than twenty, but I know a man of sense don't care for such things as that with such a fine woman."

Darcy missed his next wafer.

Manton left it up as Darcy stretched his fingers and adjusted his grip. "What then, sir?"

"The thing is, I normally wouldn't even consider a man without a title for Elizabeth. You probably guessed as much, so I thought I'd just drop a word in your ear. I hear excellent things of your estate and income, and Darcy is an old name, if an untitled one. She could do worse." He tapped Darcy on the arm jovially.

Darcy put the gun down flat on the table. Manton tactfully disappeared. "I think there's been a misunderstanding. I have no intentions toward Miss Elliot."

"Is that so? I did think perhaps you and Miss Bingley were on the way to bells, but I didn't want to hurt Elizabeth's spirits."

"As far as I am concerned, Miss Elliot has no need to stay in London."

"Well, I did think it might not be the thing, what with you having no title. Still, you are a good-looking fellow, and she could do worse."

"Yes. You said that before."

Sir Walter's attention had moved on. "I must say I don't like those boots, however. Nearly reach your knee—farmer boots, belike."

This criticism did not land. As if Darcy would copy the mode of a vain, old-fashioned baronet who lived beyond his means. "Fashion was not my aim this morning."

"Ah, well. You can lead a horse to water, as they say. Good morning, Mr. Darcy!"

Sir Walter took himself off, apparently not overly concerned at his daughter's coming disappointment.

Mr. Darcy finished shooting his twenty wafers. "Only nine of twenty," he said ruefully. "I think that is a personal *worst.*"

Manton shifted, wrinkling his tanned nose. "Everyone has those days, sir, even me."

"That's a lie. You're a genius with the designing *and* shooting of your guns."

Manton smiled, gratified. "Thank you, sir. And I may not have shot 9 of 20 since my salad days, but if I had the—er—provocation of untimely confrontations, I still might."

Darcy chuckled. "Thank you."

"Another twenty, sir? Find your balance again."

"Not today. I fear my balance won't return so easily."

# { 8 }

LIZZY WALKED THE FOOTBRIDGE over the stream with Jane and Lydia, balancing three packages in one hand and a hatbox against her hip.

"Lydia, you bought too many things."

Lydia was similarly encumbered, as was Jane, though to be fair, half the things were requests from their mother.

Lydia's purchases made it worse, however, and she'd no need to spend all her pin money in one day.

Lydia shrieked with alarm and laughter. "I nearly lost Mother's linen in the brook! Truly I did."

"If you do, *you* have to fetch it."

"There's no more water between here and home." Jane sounded unusually cross. "Here, Lydia—give me those, and I'll fit them in this satchel. Then you run up ahead and send James or Alice back to help. I'm going to wait here."

Lydia was often labeled "energetic" for a reason. "Fine! You both walk like old ladies." She tumbled her things into Jane's arms and went on.

There were several boulders on this side of the Lea, the brook that fed the lake down below, and Jane set her things on a flat space on one of the rocks. She flexed her gloved hands when they were free. Lizzy did the same, and they leaned against the hip-high boulders.

The sun was shining, and it was the warmest day they'd had in weeks, though it was the first of December. Jane didn't seem to be enjoying it.

The sound of the brook was quiet just here, and through a gap in the trees, Lizzy could see the lake reflecting the gray-blue sky.

Mr. Bingley and everyone at Netherfield had been gone for two weeks. The Friday he had told Jane he would return by had come and gone almost eight days ago.

Lizzy's reassurance that they would be back soon was starting to pall. Lizzy had assured Jane that Caroline's letter insinuating that Charles was interested in someone else was false.

"He cares about you," Lizzy had said. "It was obvious. She may be blind to it, but none of the rest of us were."

But now... it was obvious Bingley wasn't as eager to come back as they'd hoped.

Jane sighed. "I am sorry I snapped at you and Lydia."

"You didn't. Are you feeling quite the thing?"

"I am fine, it is only my own silliness about Mr. Bingley. I had hopes—*you* know. And Mother won't stop talking about him! I can bear his loss with equanimity, if only people would leave me alone about it. It is so *useless* to discuss it continually."

This was as close to a rant as Jane had ever come.

Lizzy squeezed her hand. "It is too awful. I wish I could bear it for you."

"No, you have borne enough, dear Lizzy. I know you went through much with our mother when you rejected Mr. Collins. And that was worse."

"Worse—when my heart was not at all involved? It was frustrating, but not heartbreaking."

Jane was silent for a moment, then a half-strangled sob sounded.

Lizzy wrapped her arms around Jane. "Oh, my dear."

Jane sniffed for a bit, wiping tears from her cheeks as they fell. This was the only time she had cried over her disappointed hopes since the Bingleys left. Soon however, she wiped her eyes for good. "There. I have that out of my system, and as Father likes to say, 'A girl likes to be crossed in love now and then." Jane's voice was wan and sad, but she attempted to smile.

They were composed when Lydia returned bringing James, their man-of-all-work. But along with Lydia there was a regular crowd. Mary and Kitty were with her, as well as Charlotte Lucas and the younger Elliot sisters who must have walked over to visit. Then there was also Mr. Musgrove, the Elliots' family friend.

"I have brought a parade," Lydia called. "They were all visiting, but we felt it too beautiful to stay inside. James will carry back our packages and we will take a turn around the lake."

Lizzy looked to Jane, who probably wanted to lie down after her cry, but Jane shook her head slightly. "Certainly, we can go around the lake."

Perhaps it *would* be better to walk with them, Lizzy reflected, than to entertain them in the house with her mother loudly bemoaning Bingley's abandonment.

"It *is* a lovely day," Anne said, "but if you two are tired from walking into Meryton, we can certainly go back to the house."

Mary Elliot was sullen. "*I* feel distinctly unwell to-day, Anne, but you still made *me* come. Yet the moment anyone else looks tired, you are all complaisance."

Charles Musgrove gave her his elbow. "Come, Mary, it's quite pretty, even with the leaves fallen. And you said only an hour ago that you felt perfectly well."

"I only said that because you were all so eager to visit. I could barely get a word in edgewise." She took his arm.

The oddly assorted group—almost all ladies, with the exception of Charles Musgrove—slowly filtered into pairs as they continued down the narrow walking path toward the lake.

Kitty and Mary led the way. Jane walked quietly with Anne Elliot, and Lizzy somehow fell alone to the rear of the group. Lizzy and Charlotte were still on uncertain footing with one another. Mr. Collins's presence sat like a fat specter between them. Charlotte glanced at her, then fell into step with Lydia.

Mr. Darcy would've walked with her, Lizzy thought traitorously, and then immediately banished the thought. She was not *lonely*, not among four sisters and a neighborhood she'd known her entire life. It was merely odd to have had the brief, dubious honor of holding his attention.

Just before Darcy and the Bingleys left Hertfordshire, Lizzy had realized how the wind lay, and the surprise of it had overshadowed the rest of the embarrassing evening at the Netherfield Ball.

She didn't suddenly think better of him, but she was flattered that he'd come so far from his first impression of her as to actually seek her out. Lizzy was popular and well-liked, but becoming acquainted with him was a novel experience.

Mr. Musgrove helped Mary Elliot over a tree root as they walked around the edge of the lake. She might be feeling surly, but he was enjoying himself.

Mr. Musgrove was an outdoorsman, generally liking any sport or occupation that would keep him outside the most.

He helped his father oversee the home farm in the summer. He took his fowling piece out in fall, spring, and winter if he could, and he had a good seat on a horse. If he could not be doing more, he was even happy to take a good rambling walk in the woods.

"Hertfordshire is a bit wilder than Somerset, is it not?" he said to Mary. "The skeletons of the trees stick up into the sky like—well, I need my sisters for a good metaphor, but I like the stark white and black trunks against the blue sky."

"I think I picked up a pebble in my shoe."

Mr. Musgrove held her steady while she used a finger to dislodge it from her slipper.

"You probably ought to have worn sturdier shoes."

"Well, I didn't know we were going to walk, did I? *Some* people can think of other things to do on a fine day than drag themselves through sodden leaves."

"What would you have done today?"

"Why must you and Anne always be on about getting things done? I declare, it is positively shabby-genteel the way you both harp on productivity."

"Oh, a pheasant!" he said, distracted. "Just peeked out of the bush. I wish I'd my piece with me."

She put her foot back down and tested it. "That's much better, not that you care."

"Do you get good fishing here, Miss Bennet?" he asked.

Jane did not seem to hear him, but Miss Charlotte Lucas was only a few steps behind. "They do," she told him. "My brothers come here to fish on the regular, though they say the sport this year was not as good as last."

"It never is," Mr. Musgrove said. "And do they shoot?"

"Yes, mainly on our own land, though we are such good friends with the Bennets, neither of us pay attention to the property lines."

"It is wonderful to have such neighbors; that is the kind of thing I like to see," Mr. Musgrove said. "Too many people are eager to erect fences."

"Do you go shooting often?" Charlotte asked.

"Oh, yes! My younger brother Richard will only go after deer, but I like all of it. Grouse, pheasant, hare, rabbit, deer, duck..."

"Do you hunt with horses also?"

"I've done it now and again, but I honestly prefer to be on foot."

Mary sighed. "Must we discuss the merits of walking while *walking*?"

Mr. Musgrove laughed. "I suppose not. Sorry if I am boring you, Miss Lucas."

"Not at all. Fowling is as important to women as it is to men, for the meat it introduces to the table. My father has taught my brothers to make sure they get every bird they shoot—and if we have plenty, we can give to the neighbors."

"It is an excellent way of forging good relations," Mr. Musgrove agreed. "Perhaps that is why I like it. A good walk, a bit of sport, and people smile at me when I'm done. I'm afraid I'm an amazingly simple man."

Mary murmured something under her breath that sounded like agreement.

Mr. Musgrove didn't mind her; Mary had always been like this. She was just as familiar to him as Anne, though a few years his junior. In fact, now he came to think of it, perhaps he should offer for her, if Anne would not have him.

He'd rather have Anne—much—but Mary wasn't a bad girl, just a bit crotchety when she didn't get her way.

Mary looked back at him. "What is it? Have I got a spot on my face or something?"

Charlotte continued to chat with Mr. Musgrove and Mary Elliot, and she could only think that the man was remarkably patient. Her brothers would have left the complaining Mary on her own by now, or pushed her into the lake, more likely.

Mr. Musgrove simply let it all roll past him, encouraging her at times, but seeming in no way to lose his own enjoyment of the walk from his companion's bad humor. If more men were like him, Charlotte thought, the world would be a more peaceful place.

"You'd be welcome to shoot on our preserve," Charlotte told him. "I know my father would second the invitation. He always does when anyone new is in the neighborhood."

"He already did invite me," Mr. Musgrove said. "Very affable man, your father. Reminds me of my father."

Lydia and Mary Elliot went to the side to look at the ducks, so Charlotte walked by Mr. Musgrove. She inquired after his sisters and their school situation, and from there it was short jump to his own school days. Charlotte even found herself talking about her plans for educating her own children.

"My own education was adequate but not challenging," Charlotte said. "I learned more borrowing books from Lizzy and her father than what the boys' tutor ever taught me. I hope to be prepared for my own children, both for practical learning and for books."

Mr. Musgrove kicked a branch off the path, lest it catch the ladies' skirts. "I admit I don't read as much as I ought, but I am glad I had a year at Cambridge. It did teach me quite a lot, though I daresay my profs were not impressed. At least now I do not feel such a dunce when talking with men more educated than me."

"I feel the same way about Lizzy," Charlotte said. "She can still talk circles around me and knows more classics than I ever will, but at least I can understand her. And when she needs to know how tuck a hemstitch just so, or get the chicken down into the pillow sack, she comes to me."

He laughed. "Yes. The parson will be lucky to have you and your practical wisdom."

Charlotte felt a sudden wave of coldness as she thought of Mr. Collins. Her animation died away. "I hope so."

Why could not Mr. Collins be more like Mr. Musgrove? Probably Mr. Musgrove had all sorts of flaws and failings, but he also had common sense and good nature and patience. Those alone made him a paragon of a man, in her opinion, though to add to that, he seemed intelligent enough, loyal to his family, and interested in others.

Mr. Musgrove nodded. "You will like the region, I hope. Kent is beautiful and the Downs are extraordinary. My mother likes Leeds Castle and the white cliffs of Dover, but for me it's the call of the Downs and the purple heather in the fall. You can bag thirty grouse in an afternoon there, on a good day."

*How* could Anne Elliot have refused him? Perhaps there was some other part of his character that alienated Anne—he was a drunkard or bad at dancing—but Charlotte could not imagine it.

In short, she liked him, and Charlotte was seven-and-twenty! She did not let her emotions run away with her, if she ever had done.

Lizzy passed them with a wave—she was a more vigorous walker—but Charlotte looked away.

The only thing worse than regretting her limited choices in life was having her friend guess and pity her for it.

When they returned to the house, Charlotte revised her opinion. There *were* worse things.

It was not pleasant to hear Mrs. Bennet whisper loudly to her girls, "Mr. Musgrove is worth even *more* than Mr. Bingley! They say his estate in Somerset, which he will inherit, is worth five or six thousand a year. Not as much as Mr. Darcy, but he is so much more agreeable." She suddenly stopped and glared at Lizzy. "If you *dare* turn him away like you did Mr. Collins, I will turn you out, Lizzy. I swear it! You have been stubborn, and I have borne it with amazing patience, despite the damage to my nerves. If you reject yet another eligible man, I won't be answerable for the consequences!"

"Mother," Lizzy hissed. "He is in the room, and I am almost certain he followed the *Elliots* to the neighborhood. His interest lies with them."

Mrs. Bennet had sniffed. "Well, Mr. Collins came to offer for you, yet Charlotte stole him from under your nose. Who is to say the same might not happen with Mr. Musgrove?"

Lizzy winced. "Let us please talk about something else."

Mrs. Bennet threw up her hands. "It is not as if I *wish* to make such plans, but none of you has the least foresight! I must plan everything, and it not so easy on my nerves, I can tell you. I had a most alarming spasm last night. Your father declared it was the worst I've ever had, and he moved to the spare room so that I might stretch out on the bed."

"That was considerate," Jane said.

"Yes, he is an excellent father to you girls. Did he not visit the Longs and invite Mr. Musgrove to visit within the week? You see, he *does* love you after all, and it is *wickedly* ungrateful not to appreciate it."

# { 9 }

WICKHAM TRIED TO KISS MARY ELLIOT under the stairs at Lucas Lodge, but she was more tiresome than Georgiana Darcy had been.

Georgiana was young and uncertain, but she had not been coy or teasing in the way Mary thought was alluring.

Mary turned her face away and put her gloved hand over his lips. "You really ought not. Didn't your mother teach you manners?"

He kissed her hand. "She did, and I have followed every one of them."

"You are very dreadful, Wickham, admit it."

"Only if you *like* dreadful. For I cannot live without you, Mary. Whatever I am, I must have you."

She blushed and pulled her hand away. "You're trying to turn my head, sir, but you have not yet succeeded."

He *had* succeeded, she just didn't know it yet. "Then tell me what I have to do. What impresses the beautiful Mary Elliot? I know I am worthless compared to you. I have nothing to offer but my heart."

She thrilled at his words; he could tell. He tried again, and she didn't turn away.

Wickham was good. With any luck he could get her father to agree, or if not, perhaps a runaway situation would work as well. He felt Mary was only a month or two from being willing to run away with him, if needed.

Kissing her was distracting, at any event. Wickham never had to pretend about that.

He was startled when Lizzy Bennet cleared her throat.

Mary flushed red and blotchy, pulling away from him. "I was only—don't say anything to Anne!"

"Of course not, it's none of my business," Lizzy said. "However I was asked to fetch more cards for Lady Lucas, and she has a stash in that cupboard." Lizzy nodded beyond them. "Er—perhaps, Miss Elliot, you ought to run upstairs and... tidy up before Lady Lucas sets out the games."

Mary huffed. She went around to the front side of the staircase and disappeared up it.

Wickham straightened the sleeve of his red coat, which Mary had mangled. "Good evening."

He was a little discomposed that it would be *her* who stumbled upon them, but not unduly. He had outfaced far worse.

She was looking at him with narrowed eyes.

"Please don't sketch a portrait of my character from this one moment," Wickham said. "I know it reflects poorly on me, but I am not normally this forward. You may ask anyone in town, everyone will confirm I never step a toe out of line."

"You must know I can't ask that sort of question all over town."

"You might ask a few friends."

"I will. You are still blocking the cupboard, sir."

"I apologize." He spread his hands as he moved. "What can I say? The best of us is sometimes overwhelmed by temptation."

She turned back toward the Lucases' drawing room with a woven wicker basket filled with small decks of cards. "And Mary Elliot offered overwhelming temptation?"

"What are you saying?" Wickham acted hurt. "You would insult Miss Mary's appearance?"

Lizzy held the door for him to the bright drawing room, shutting it firmly behind them. The noise of the

Lucas home wrapped around them, and it was never less than pandemonium.

"I am not insulting *Mary* at all," Lizzy said. "She is not, I don't feel, an instigator. I am doubting that she would have pursued that moment on her own."

"I agree, she could not have pursued that moment on her own, she would look very silly under the stairs by herself in such case."

Lizzy laughed, though his comment was inappropriate. "You know that isn't what I meant."

Wickham grinned. Anyone he could make laugh was halfway won. "I meant her no harm, and no harm has come to her."

"We'll see. Please keep in mind that I know every house in these parts as if it is my own. Most of the hostesses feel I am a second daughter, and they do not hesitate to send me on quick errands. Unfortunately, I run across such moments rather often. You might keep it in mind."

"I will endeavor not to put you to the blush again."

"Yes, observe me in a feminine quake."

He laughed. "Bravo, last word."

Lizzy did not take her accidental discovery as lightly as she pretended, though with the prevalence with which she was finding couples in intimate moments, perhaps she should have.

She *did* attempt to find out a little more about Wickham, but she was disappointed. All she got were gossipy versions of the story he himself had told: A devoted mentor, a jealous and vindictive Darcy, a lost living.

What Wickham did after that event, which must have been at least five or six years ago, if not more, was unknown. Even Lizzy's Aunt Phillips knew little, though she had the most embellished version of the Darcy story, now complete with a wicked stepmother.

The only new information Lizzy received was from her Uncle Phillips, who only said, "Wickham? He's run up the devil of a tab at the shop, I hope he's good for it."

Somehow the very sameness of the story she heard made her doubt it even further. Mr. Darcy was proud and disagreeable at times, but she'd seen hints of humor and a sense of justice that didn't fit with it.

Perhaps if *she* had been the one Wickham sought out, his flattery would have been enough to sell his sob-story. It was an ignominious thought, and Lizzy didn't flay herself by pursuing it very far.

She seriously considered telling Anne Elliot about her younger sister's questionable choices, but on thinking it over, Lizzy could not reconcile going back on her word. Nor was she a tattle-tale, if the situation did not demand it.

Instead, she endeavored to have a private conversation with Mary Elliot the next time they were all at Longbourn.

Lydia and Kitty were ensconced at the kitchen table with bonnets, feathers, fake flowers, and ribbons. There were yeasted rolls baking in the kitchen, and Lizzy was already hungry for dinner.

When the Elliots arrived with Charlotte—who did not even give Lizzy a small smile!—Lizzy requested Mary Elliot accompany her to take a message to the farm.

It was clear Mary was about to scornfully decline, but Lizzy gave her a significant look, raising her eyebrows and shifting her gaze between Mary and Anne.

"Yes, fine," Mary said. "*Another* walk, lovely."

To fortify her for an unpleasant conversation, Lizzy took Mary out by way of the kitchen. She took a roll for each of them before they left. It was not a frigid day, for there was almost no wind, but there were thick clouds and a still, cold chill.

The warm bread in their hands helped a little.

Mary sniffed. "We never steal bread from the kitchen at Kellynch."

"That's a pity. It's one of life's great pleasures."

The home farm was not very near, but the byre Lizzy was heading for was only half a mile away. They took the path in the opposite direction from the lake, and it was less beautiful than the other. The bushes were prickly and almost bare, though at least the path was dry, and the muddy spots had crusted over.

"Well, what is it?" Mary said. "I assume you did not particularly *want* to take this walk, unless you too have an unhealthy obsession with fresh air."

"Guilty as charged," Lizzy said. "But yes. I have done some discreet inquiring about Lieutenant Wickham, and I must confess, something feels off."

"I *knew* it was that. Why do older sisters feel such a need to interfere? Do you do this with your own sisters?"

"No—well, not really. Lydia would not listen to me, and I have my doubts about Mary and Kitty. But I think you are more mature than my sisters, so in a way, this is a compliment."

"*Charmed*, I'm sure."

"You are also in a more dangerous situation than my sisters, because you are the daughter of a wealthy baronet. It is an unhappy truth that money begets nearly as many problems as poverty. Different problems, but problems, nonetheless."

"You would say Wickham wants our money? No, I think I know a cad when I meet one. He certainly didn't kiss me like he didn't care! You don't understand. No one ever likes me for me—I'm the young one, the sickly one. But Wickham *does* like me! Father's favorite is

Elizabeth, and Mother's favorite, I'm told, was Anne. I'm not as pretty as Elizabeth, or as energetic as either of them, and it is not *fair*."

There was enough hurt in this immature speech to wring Lizzy's heart. Knowing that she herself was her father's favorite, it also triggered guilt. Did her own sisters harbor the same feeling—that their father favored Lizzy, their mother favored Lydia, and there was nothing left for them?

Lizzy shook her head. "I hope you will live to find that *many* people care about you for yourself. Certainly Anne does, I've seen it! Mr. Musgrove as well. Wickham may even be one of those people. I certainly don't know everything; I would just warn you to be a *little* on your guard."

Perhaps with another sort of girl this warning might have been given and received in the spirit it was meant, but Mary was not that girl. Possibly there was no eighteen-year-old who would've taken it well, Lizzy mused.

"Now that you have insulted me *and* Wickham, can we turn back? I have no desire to visit your wretched byre merely to be insulted further on the way back. Or perhaps you wanted Wickham for yourself, and you are merely jealous that he has pursued *me*."

Mary expounded in this vein—the one most in line with her own wishes—and Lizzy tried to contain her annoyance. Perhaps she had overstepped. She knew nothing essential about Wickham except that he'd been indiscreet about his background, and that he'd gotten into some debt in town.

Charlotte Lucas sat at the messy table at Longbourn, and avoided Lizzy's eyes when they returned.

Heretofore Charlotte was the one who would go with Lizzy on errands. It hurt to see how their friendship had broken, but Charlotte had walked into it with her eyes wide open.

Charlotte rolled up a wide brown ribbon and used a small string to tie it in a neat roll. Then she started on a thin scarlet one. The Bennet worktable was always a mess; she could not help tidying it.

Charlotte had known when she accepted Mr. Collins right after Lizzy rejected him, that it would not be ideal for their friendship. She had *not* quite expected the scorn that Lizzy felt for him, or that that scorn would extend to Charlotte. Lizzy had such lofty standards for love and marriage.

Charlotte had reduced the chaos on the table to manageable proportions when the Bennets' footman, James, announced another visitor, Mr. Musgrove.

Charlotte felt color in her cheeks, and was glad she sat near the kitchen, where the warmth of the air might account for it. She was avoiding Mr. Musgrove as best she could, but there was not much she could do in a small, interconnected neighborhood with limited entertainment.

It was worse when he came and sat between her and Lydia—though to be fair, there was an empty chair there. He turned to her and smiled. "Good afternoon, Miss Lucas! I trust your sister Emily is over her sore throat?"

"Not quite, but thank you for asking. She has passed it to Jack and Harriet, so my mother is busy with them."

"Oh, that's unfortunate, sorry to hear it."

And he *was* sorry, she could tell. He was always kind to her young siblings. He was a stupidly kind person, and she could see him being an excellent father. Not doting, probably, but caring and consistent.

"And have you heard from your sisters?" Charlotte asked. "Are they home yet?"

"Why, yes! Louisa has just written to say that I must return soon. They are ready for the Christmas season, and apparently it is not quite right if I am not there."

"That is a compliment to you."

"I think it is more a recognition that I'm the one who will cut the holly boughs and squire them to all the balls in the neighborhood. They must have practiced dancing more with me than with their dancing master at this point. My mother is in no rush to marry them off, but they are eager to enjoy their first season."

"From your tone, I gather you do not enjoy it?"

"I'm just indulging a touch of pettiness. Uppercross is an excellent neighborhood. I never meet a man except he becomes a friend. I'd just rather spend time with my friends in the fields or woods, not in the ballroom."

"But I assume there are fewer ladies in the fields."

"Yes, true. I'd hoped that this year... never mind. I don't make friends as easily with the ladies I meet. I'm only comfortable with those I grew up with." He nodded toward Mary and Anne Elliot.

"You seem comfortable with me, Mr. Musgrove."

His eyes widened. "Why, that is so!"

Charlotte suddenly recollected herself. She was perilously close to *flirting*. "I daresay it is because I am engaged and—and at least several years your senior."

"That didn't help me with—"

He was interrupted by a question from Mary Elliot.

Charlotte surreptitiously pressed a cold hand to her warm cheek. It was best that she was engaged before she met Mr. Musgrove, otherwise her preference for him would have given real pain, rather than just this ache. Even if she was unattached, there was no way he would have proposed to her. She was seven-and-twenty. She was plain. She came from undistinguished, genteelly impoverished stock.

This was for the best.

*Starch and Strategy*

Charlotte rose to collect all the rolls of ribbon into the basket.

# { 10 }

DARCY FOUND THE PREPONDERANCE of mirrors in Sir Walter Elliot's townhouse to be off-putting.

Everywhere Darcy turned he was confronted with his own image. His profile outlined against a dark wood door, his glance between the sconces—and though Darcy did not mean to keep staring at himself in the mirrors—it was surprisingly hard to ignore himself.

Darcy was surprised at his expression—did he always look so stoic and uninterested at parties? Or was that the fault of Sir Walter and Miss Elliot? Darcy's own mental image of himself did not involve such a clenched jaw, flattened mouth, and hard eyes.

Was this how he looked in Hertfordshire at all those dreadful country parties? No wonder Bingley had remonstrated with him about his manner.

Such reflections, though perhaps showing a step in the direction of self-awareness and a willingness to change, were useless tonight. He did not *want* to encourage Sir Walter or Miss Elliot.

He'd told Sir Walter, of course, that Miss Elliot was not to expect an offer from him. The Elliots had not yet left town, however, and Miss Elliot's invitation to her small party had been made official with a printed invitation.

Darcy planned to cry off, but Bingley forestalled him. "Come on, you must not make me go alone with Caroline. Miss Elliot intimidates me! I know she would never deign to marry someone like me, but if she suddenly took the notion into her head, I fear I should find myself committed before I realized what had happened."

"If she drags you to Gretna Green, I'll rescue you in high style. This party, however..."

"One might even say that you *owe* me a favor," Bingley interrupted.

So Darcy was here, but as every reflective surface showed, under protest.

Miss Bingley seemed to sense his mood, for she came to join him. She tugged gently on an evening glove that went past her elbow, positioning it just right. "You do not have to endure Miss Elliot just to babysit Charles."

"Nor do you." From this part of the room, there was one mirror reflecting his own face along with the back of Caroline's dress. It was high-waisted and tied with a lavender ribbon which hung down her back. He could also see her profile in a different mirror—this one an oval.

Her expression was intent, hopeful—if he had ever seen such an expression on Jane Bennet's face toward Bingley, he would have been convinced of her affection.

Darcy was frustrated with himself. Why did he *not* want to marry Caroline? She was handsome, worldly, a friend... She was not vain and empty-headed like Miss Elliot. Caroline was proud, but she was also well educated, intelligent, and accomplished.

But he did not want to marry her. He could not imagine waking with her at Pemberley, drinking coffee in the morning, planning a Christmas party over dinner, or playing chess in the evening.

"You must not grip that wine glass any tighter or you will break it." Caroline nodded at the stem that was in his flexing fingers.

"Of course."

Caroline held out her hand for his empty glass, and he handed it to her. She crossed the room and set his and hers on the edge of the table to be cleared.

Miss Elliot came up to her. Her eyes were glittering. "I wish you luck."

Caroline looked around. "With the game of picquet? Do you wish me to play?"

"No. With *Darcy*. My father spoke with him last week, and he found out Darcy has a prior interest. I can only assume it is you."

The glitter in Miss Elliot's eyes now made sense. Was she angry?

Caroline's heart thrilled. "Darcy said he was attached to me? When?"

"He may as well have. He made it clear he was not interested in *me*, and my father could only conclude from his manner that he had a prior attachment, or possibly even a secret engagement."

Caroline tilted her head in confusion. "With me?"

"I assumed so. If not you, then who? He seemed rather friendly with that girl in Hertfordshire, but surely he can do better than that."

"She doesn't mean anything."

Miss Elliot shrugged, though she did not look perfectly reconciled. "Does she not?"

Caroline was not reconciled either.

THE FOLLOWING DAY, CAROLINE went riding with Mr. Darcy.

The clouds had broken, and a watery December sunshine filled Hyde Park. Most of the flowers were shriveled along the pathways, but a few hearty purple blooms lingered.

Several chestnut trees added a splash of lingering red and orange leaves against the gray of bare branches and the green of pines. The carriageway was not packed as it would be in May, but there was a steady clip of phaetons, curricles, and even a four-horse racing carriage.

Mr. Darcy looked dashing in his green riding coat, and Caroline was pleased to be seen riding with him. People might well assume there was a future between them.

Having already discussed the weather, Charles's distracted and sad air at breakfast, and Darcy's plan for Georgiana's winter, Caroline ventured to less firm territory. "I believe Miss Elliot will not be tormenting you any longer."

"Thankfully she does not occupy enough of my mind or calendar to truly torment me."

"She is under the impression that you have a prior interest. She even alighted on Lizzy Bennet in her speculation. Can you imagine?"

"An odd surmise, certainly."

"You can picture my laughter. A completely unsuitable family for Charles, let alone for *you.*"

Darcy's expression was not welcoming, but the subject was now like a scab that she could not resist peeling, even though she sensed how much it would hurt. "The easiest way to avoid such scandals would be to announce an engagement before you bring out Georgiana next year."

"Thank you for your advice, but I would never let gossip force me into action." He paused as they passed another lady and gentleman on horses, nodding to one another. He continued. "We've been friends for some time, Caroline, so I think I ought to be frank with you. If you are in some fashion waiting for me—if you have hopes or expectations, however unexpressed—I must urge you to look elsewhere."

Caroline caught her breath, her cheeks blossoming with painful color. Her crushing disappointment made her unwise. "I suppose I ought to say I have no idea what you're talking about—but surely we are better friends than that. May I inquire why you are so certain—when we have been friends these three years? Is it my birth? You are fine with Charles as a friend, but the future Mrs. Darcy must be above reproach?"

"I don't deserve that accusation, and it is beneath you to give it. I have never once belittled your background. I don't care about a woman's status."

"Then why *not* me—what else is there?"

He frowned. "Beyond birth and status? There are many things. I respect you, but I do not think we should suit."

"Take care. If you go about with that attitude, you'll contract a worse alliance than we saved Charles from."

"In fact, my choices are less limited than your brother's. Where he might need to take a care, I do not."

Shocked and angry, Caroline mocked, "Ah, then you *are* thinking about Lizzy Bennet. I do beg your pardon, but your trenchant remarks about her mother mislead me."

He shook his head. "I have no intention of offering for her. Does *every* woman assume a man would propose unless he had a prior commitment? You are acting like Miss Elliot."

Caroline's stomach clenched. She felt as if she had been punched. Her horse shied nervously, and Darcy put a heavy hand on the base of its neck, just above her hands, to calm it. "I apologize, Caroline, that was badly put. I was trying to be honest. This coming season, you should look about you for a man you care about."

"I care about you."

"I think we should ride back."

Caroline's vulnerability, thus thrown back in her face, turned quickly to anger.

That afternoon, she wrote a note to Miss Elliot.

*Starch and Strategy*

The following morning, she received a reply.

*Dear Miss Bingley,*

*Why, yes, I would be delighted to have a friend accompany me to Bath! My father and I both adore you, you know, and you have all my sympathy at Mr. D's terrible behavior. How dare he lead you on so! We plan to leave London on Thursday at noon, if you will be so good as to arrive promptly by eleven.*

*Your friend,*

*Elizabeth Elliot*

# { 11 }

LIZZY FROZE AS SHE APPROACHED the coat closet between the dining room and Mrs. Long's front door.

Another couple dallying in the dark? She was beginning to think the entire neighborhood was engaged in clandestine caressing.

When several of the party at Mrs. Long's house had complained that they could hardly see the table for playing cards, Lizzy had volunteered to fetch another lamp for Mrs. Long—an amiable if absent-minded lady.

Two people were clearly in the coat room, and their shadows were cast in blurry fashion on the great carved wood surface of the main door. Lizzy would probably have ignored them, but her errand was to fetch the spare lamp from the entryway, and it was nowhere in sight. In fact, the two unknown people had apparently taken it with them.

Lizzy cleared her throat and came around the corner.

To her shock, it was Charlotte and Mr. Musgrove.

They were not embracing, but they *were* standing rather near one another. The spare lamp was in Charlotte's hand, and Mr. Musgrove was sorting through an alarming pile of knitted scarves, hats, and gloves.

He looked around cheerfully at her. "Hullo, Miss Lizzy. I was trying to find my new gloves to show the pattern to Miss Lucas, but they have gotten mixed in with my cousins' gloves. It is a very nice pattern, knitted by my mother."

Charlotte, on the other hand, looked rather red in the low light. "Yes! That's all." She held up the lamp so he could see better. "You know I was never happy with the set of the fingers from the pattern I used last winter."

"Er, I do recall something about that," Lizzy said. The picture they made was entirely innocent, except for Charlotte's flushed face.

Mr. Musgrove stood up straight, triumphant. "A-ha! Here they are."

He beamed at them both and pressed the brown wool items into Charlotte's free hand. "You must take them as long as you need, I can make do for a few days."

"I wouldn't want you to be cold on my account. If I can sketch the outline and record the number of stitches this evening, I shall be happy." Her plain face glowed in the low light.

Lizzy stood there stupidly until Charlotte side-stepped past her to get out the door. "Did you need something, Lizzy?"

"I—I needed the lamp. For the table. In the drawing room."

Charlotte handed it to Mr. Musgrove. "Would you take the lamp back for us? I'll be there directly, after we fetch a blank sheet of paper for this pattern. I know Mrs. Long would not begrudge me a piece."

He obliged, and Lizzy trailed Charlotte up the stairs. Charlotte was no longer red, but pale.

"There was nothing untoward, just now," Charlotte said. "You looked so shocked, but Mr. Musgrove was just being friendly. He heard me bemoaning the new pattern printed in the *Ladies' Bazaar*, and he could not praise his mother's highly enough. He wanted to show me."

"I would never think badly of you, Charlotte. You don't owe me an explanation."

Charlotte opened the door to the children's room and went to the desk in the corner. "Wouldn't you? I believe you've thought quite badly of me since Mr. Collins's visit."

"Not badly! I promise. I was shocked, and I spoke harshly." Lizzy shook her head. It was not Mr. Collins she was picturing just now. "But Charlotte, do you...care about Mr. Musgrove?"

"No. Don't be silly, Lizzy. I am engaged, however much you might dislike it."

"I deserved that. But, as my best and oldest friend, just tell me, *do* you care about him?"

Charlotte suddenly dashed a hand to her brown eyes, wiping away tears. "No."

She wrenched open the desk drawer and got out a piece of hot-press paper. Her wet fingers got spots on it.

"Oh, dash it all." She dropped the paper on the desk and pressed her hand to her eyes. "You push too hard. What do you want me to say? That you were right? Yes, I like Mr. Musgrove, but it is meaningless. He wouldn't have offered for me anyway, and I in *no way* regret accepting Mr. Collins. Happiness in marriage is en-entirely a matter of chance." Her often repeated maxim was less resolute when she was crying.

Lizzy wrapped her arms around Charlotte, who leaned her head against Lizzy's shoulder and sobbed.

"I'm sorry, Charlotte. I'm so sorry." Lizzy wasn't sure whether she was apologizing for how harsh she'd been about Mr. Collins, or for the larger predicament that Charlotte found herself in. "Just breathe."

Charlotte's sadness subsided, and she squeezed Lizzy in thanks before pulling away to dry her eyes. "Ugh, I must look a *sight*, and I can't even disappear. I have to go home soon."

"You'll be just fine in a few minutes. We'll tell Mrs. Long we couldn't immediately find a paper."

Lizzy said nothing else about Mr. Musgrove. It would only hurt Charlotte.

When Lizzy mentally contrasted Mr. Collins with Mr. Musgrove, it hurt her too.

Mr. Musgrove was not Lizzy's ideal man—if she even had one—but he was a jovial, kind gentleman, full of common sense and a love of sport. He was, in fact, perfect for Charlotte!

A string of *if only* thoughts unrolled in her mind's eye, and it made her angry. Did Providence reserve no happy endings for Hertfordshire? Jane, Charlotte, Lizzy, Mary Elliot...

Lizzy followed Charlotte back to the parlor thinking dangerous thoughts.

When she passed the coat closet again, she was almost certain she heard Wickham's laugh and Mary's murmur. Lizzy ignored them.

THAT NIGHT, WHEN THE BENNETS had returned through the frosty night to the welcome warmth of

Longbourn, Lizzy's mother called her into her bedchamber.

She was propped against the headboard with quantities of pillows, and she had already changed into her nightwear, with a cap tied over her lightly graying hair. She was plump, which had staved off the onset of many wrinkles, but now there were several deep lines between her eyes.

"I am feeling quite feverish and queer, and *poor* Lydia is not feeling at all well either. I am afraid we were *exposed* to something at the Longs' house tonight. I cannot like the Long girls. They are quite fast, and dare I say, vulgar. They are *just* the sort to give me a nasty fever."

Interpreting this—for Mrs. Long was a close friend and her daughters were humble, good-natured girls—Lizzy sighed. "Did they say something about Mr. Musgrove?"

"I'm sure I don't care, for *you* certainly won't make a push to attach him. I did think maybe Lydia... but all Mr. Musgrove will do is find mittens for Charlotte and dance attendance on the Long girls. Shameless!"

"They are his cousins. Er, second cousins, I think."

"It is very unlucky to stay with cousins, especially when they are so *pushing*. I have no opinion of them."

"Comfort yourself, ma'am, he won't marry them. I'd be shocked if he made either of his cousins an offer."

*If only he would make Charlotte an offer,* Lizzy couldn't help thinking, but she knew that was unfair. For all Mr. Musgrove knew, Charlotte was happily engaged.

But then, why must a previous engagement stop a possible love match? Women jilted men for far less every day. Not women like Charlotte, though.

Lizzy was startled when her mother's mind seemed to follow hers.

"I don't like it," she was saying. "Charlotte stole Mr. Collins out from under our noses, and now she is employing her wiles on Mr. Musgrove. I never would have thought it of her."

"Charlotte has *no* wiles," Lizzy said. "You mustn't say things that might hurt her reputation."

Mrs. Bennet sniffed. "I'm sure I don't envy Lady Lucas. If Charlotte is not pursuing Mr. Musgrove, she has turned into a terrible flirt. And at her age! At seven-and-twenty, she ought to be settled down and having babies."

"Charlotte did not flirt with him at all! He is just a friendly man. You could as well say he flirted with you."

Charlotte *did* look at him in a warm way, however, and Lizzy wished her mother had not noticed it.

"Well, I hope no more wealthy gentlemen will come into the neighborhood, for it brings out the worst in one's neighbors. It is such a *trial* to have integrity."

She waved Lizzy away, and Lizzy retreated gratefully to her bed, with a brick warming the foot of her mattress from underneath.

Lizzy, when once she began to think about seriously disrupting people's lives, found it both terrifying and addicting.

For why should she stop with Charlotte? If she was willing to transgress society's taboos in a small way or two—for the greater good!—why not see what could be done for Jane and Bingley also? Perhaps at the same time she could spare Mary Elliot an embarrassing and painful interlude with Lieutenant Wickham.

After a night of thinking, Lizzy's goals, along with the sun on her walk to Meryton, rose to extraordinary, buttery heights.

The more Lizzy considered Wickham's behavior: his determination with Mary Elliot, his complete willingness to slander Mr. Darcy, and his practiced sighs and downcast looks, the less she trusted him.

That was her first task this morning, and after a quick trip to her Uncle Phillips's shop, she headed toward the post office.

Two letters rested in her bag. One was written by her uncle.

*To Mr. Darcy,*

*Please excuse my forwardness in writing to you, sir, but I have inquiries to make about one George Wickham. He has run up some debts in my store, as well as several other establishments of Meryton. If you have any information on his habits and his likelihood of payment, particularly if he has committed crimes of monetary or other sort in another district, I would appreciate the information. I would not apply to you, except that Wickham has been quite free in using your name and asserting that you are familiar with his family and history. He has said some other things, but I don't give any heed to 'em—clearly he is insulting his betters, no matter what my wife says.*

*Again, please don't take my writing as an impertinence. My niece recommended it, and I thought it worth trying your patience.*

*Yours, etc.*

*J. Phillips*

Lizzy had not particularly wanted her uncle to mention *her* involvement, but he had taken her suggestion and written the letter, so she could not be too picky.

She was not certain that Darcy would respond to this letter, but it was a worthy opening salvo. Her goals, she had decided, were threefold.

To see what could be done for Charlotte with Mr. Musgrove.

To bring Bingley back to Hertfordshire for Jane.

To save Mary Elliot—petty though she was—from Wickham.

In addition to the letter from her uncle, Lizzy carried a letter from herself to Caroline Bingley. It was one of the most awful things she had ever written, yet the words had flowed with wicked delight.

*My dear Miss Bingley,*

*Although we have not exchanged letters, Jane has shared with me your exceedingly kind and newsy messages from town, and thus I have taken the liberty to write to you.*

*I am deeply concerned. It seemed to us that there might be an understanding between you and Mr. Darcy—or perhaps, that one might come soon. Unfortunately, I must tell you I have heard the most alarming things about him.*

*It seems he was vilely cruel to the son of his father's late steward and denied the generous inheritance his father intended for young Mr. Wickham. In fact, flying in the face of all paternal loyalty, he gave the church living to another man, when it should have set up Mr. Wickham for life.*

*Of course, you are free to ignore this, but it is widely known here, and I could not but warn you. You were so kind to Jane and me while you were here, and if I can in any way repay that, I would do so. I would hate to see anyone trapped in marriage to a man devoid of honesty or integrity.*

*I also fear, perhaps, that this stain on Mr. Darcy is coloring the neighborhood's view of your brother, so perhaps it is for the best that none of you plan to return to Netherfield. Jane tells me that you suspect Charles will let the house go when his rental time is up; otherwise, I would never hint such a thing.*

*Wishing you all the best,*
*Elizabeth Bennet*

Wild horses would not drag Caroline Bingley back to Netherfield if she thought Lizzy *wanted* it, but Lizzy suspected the reverse might prove beyond her self-control. Caroline would be itching with anger at this collection of false accusations. And to be told she was *un*wanted would hopefully fill the cup of her wrath and bring her back to Netherfield in high dudgeon.

Lizzy felt no qualms at passing on the gossip about Mr. Darcy. She suspected Wickham's story to be untrue, or at least embellished, and most likely Caroline *knew* it to be untrue. Therefore, Lizzy was not actually damaging Mr. Darcy's reputation or their possible relationship.

And of course, Lizzy knew that Caroline might show her letter immediately to Darcy or Bingley, but that was all to the better.

Lizzy did not believe Wickham's sob-story, not altogether, but she had not lied about Wickham staining Darcy's reputation in the district. Perhaps her letter would lend weight to her uncle's letter, though slightly confusing for Mr. Darcy.

And the biggest hope of all: it might bring Bingley back into the neighborhood to clear his own—and probably Darcy's—good name! With any luck, Wickham would be discredited, and Mary Elliot would realize he was not to be trusted.

Lizzy mailed the letters with a smile and not the faintest hint of guilt.

On the way home, as if Providence was now assisting her with a lavish hand, she fell in with Mr. Musgrove and his cousins.

His was the more delicate case. The strategy for the two letters had presented itself last night, but unfortunately, they didn't bring Charlotte any closer to happiness.

The first order of business must be to decide if Mr. Musgrove felt any affection or interest in Charlotte. Sadly, it was entirely possible that Charlotte's feelings were one-sided. If so, Lizzy would drop this and support her friend as best she could.

When Lizzy fell in with the Longs, she easily lengthened her stride to walk next to Mr. Musgrove.

"How do you do today, sir? Will you stay much longer in Hertfordshire? I'm afraid you must be missing your home."

"Do you know, not as much as I often do! Lovely district this, and good pheasant shooting. I bagged three in an hour yesterday, and I am not a crack shot, so that was quite a pleasure!" His smile fit perfectly in his square face.

"I'm glad you are comfortable. Mrs. Long is a good hostess, and of course, you already have friends here in Anne and Mary Elliot. I hear you are often shooting near Lucas Lodge."

"Lovely family, the Lucases. Feel as if I've grown up with them. Very welcoming. Miss Lucas tells me you and she are good friends as well."

"Oh, Charlotte is a gem."

"Certainly. That parson—Collins, was it?—is a lucky man."

This could be a mere pleasantry, but Lizzy took it as a good sign. She loved Charlotte, but the fact was that no men in Hertfordshire had offered for her. None, presumably, cared if she married or died an old maid.

Mr. Musgrove's compliment was therefore unique in Lizzy's experience.

"Mr. Collins *is* a lucky man. Though, er, I am not sure he knows it. They were not acquainted very long." This was dangerous territory, and Lizzy couldn't help checking that the other boisterous family members were involved in their own conversations.

"Ah, well, he is in for a pleasant surprise."

Lizzy bit her lip. "I only hope Charlotte is as pleasantly surprised. Mr. Collins is—well, I ought not talk about him."

Mr. Musgrove's brow furrowed.

Lizzy felt she had given him enough to think on for now. "Will you shoot more pheasant today, sir, or do you give your shotgun a rest?"

# { 12 }

CAROLINE MADE A LOUD NOISE of contempt when she read Lizzy's letter, loud enough that she startled herself.

Charles looked up from the morning paper with a raised eyebrow. "Choke on a raisin? Nearly did so myself, they're like pebbles this morning."

"I didn't choke," Caroline pushed her teacup and saucer away and held the offensive letter in two fingers. "I am—disgusted by this letter."

"I daresay you got some—ahem—phlegm on it just now, but that's not the letter's fault."

"*Charles.*"

He laughed at his own impertinence. "I'm sorry, Caroline. What troubles you?"

It was at this moment that her reasons for keeping all Hertfordshire news away from her brother returned to her mind. She had been suppressing all news from

Meryton and those families, and particularly any news of Jane's letters or the Bennet family. Charles had a way of sighing and staring into the fire that did not bode well.

But she was angry, rightfully so, at the incredible impudence and vulgarity of this letter. Something really had to be done.

"It's—Well—" As she glanced over it again, the phrases about her possible relationship with Darcy were nearly galling in their bitterness. Then there was the paragraph about Darcy being a man lacking integrity and honor. The sheer audacity! She would like to show *him* this letter.

As for Bingley not to be welcome in his *own* house and neighborhood...

Caroline was too angry to speak. She tossed the letter across the table toward Charles.

He picked it up and read curiously, and then settled it flat on the table, leaning forward to read it again.

"What rot!" he said finally. "I can hardly believe it."

Caroline was relieved to hear this perfectly appropriate response; his long silence had made her nervous. "Exactly. I am sorry to have shown you, but Lizzy always was an impertinent, pushing sort of girl. I am not so shocked about *that* as the slander involved—"

"Impertinent? I think this is a very thoughtful letter. She is completely wrong about Darcy, of course, but she doesn't know that. Wickham is the worst sort of liar, Darcy tells me. This must be dealt with, of course. But it was good of her to try to warn you; the impulse was warm."

Caroline's throat closed up with suppressed anger. If Lizzy's impulse had been warm, then pigs could fly.

Charles cleared his throat. "She says you've—er—written to Jane?"

Caroline fixed him with a glare. "That is not the point. How *dare* she insinuate that we would not be welcome in Hertfordshire? It is ridiculous. The neighborhood would be *lucky* if you made Netherfield your home."

His lip quirked. "Weren't you telling me how much you disliked the district? You had all but convinced me to give it up at the end of the first six-month lease."

"I *still* think so, and you *ought* to give it up. But it is still so provoking!" She took a deep breath. "You see why I didn't like the society there. They are ready to believe any ill-founded slander no matter the source. Surely we can do better than that! In fact, I think you should write the lender and end your tenancy as soon as possible. Neither of us needs to return to such a vile town."

He smiled a little wider. "On the contrary, I feel I have an obligation to go back and clear things up a trifle. This seems the sort of thing a responsible gentleman would nip in the bud at once. I'm certain our father would have said so."

"But they are not worth your time! I'm sure Mr. Darcy would agree."

"My time is all but worthless in town, and Darcy agrees with me on *that*. He is so blasted efficient he supervises Pemberley and half his other houses from town. What exactly do you think *I* would be sacrificing?"

"At least—at least ask him," Caroline said. "He deserves to be involved in this conversation."

"I don't need to ask my friend for permission to go to a house I've rented."

"No, but it is his reputation that's been maligned."

Charles finally stopped smiling so cheerfully. "That's true. Fine, I'll talk to him."

It wasn't until later, when Charles was explaining the situation to Darcy as they walked to White's for dinner, that he realized Caroline had avoided telling him about her correspondence with Jane.

Ah, well, perhaps that was for the best, though he did want to know if Jane had asked about him. If he went back to Hertfordshire, he would be able to catch up with Jane himself.

The thought nearly had him whistling.

"You look quite cheerful at the thought of my defamation," Darcy said. They walked in step down the sidewalk of Bond Street. Passersby made way for them.

Bingley wiped his smile away. "Sorry. Wickham is a wastrel, and it's a nightmare you have to deal with him again. But it won't be that hard to fix, will it?"

"If I'm inclined to fix it. It is not my concern what people believe."

Bingley stared at him. "That is the most hypocritical thing I have ever heard you say. Have you not warned me to take care how I make people talk? Even when I was just being silly with the blokes at Cambridge, it was all 'Bingley, take care what people think of you!' And only last month you were saying I shouldn't 'sully the name my father worked for' with a perfectly respectable girl from a country family—" Bingley broke off, startled by his own anger.

Darcy had the goodness to wince. "Perhaps it sounds hypocritical, but your situation is more delicate than mine. You have to take more care than I do. Everyone I care about knows Wickham is a liar, and those who don't—are not my problem."

"Not everyone *I* care about knows it. I was wrong, you're not hypocritical, you're arrogant."

He and Darcy were silent under the weight of this— the first time Bingley had knowingly insulted his friend. Bingley did not take it back. "You don't care that Wickham is imposing on a whole community—pretending to be someone he's not? You don't care that some of those people are transferring the taint to Caroline and me? You don't care that you and Georgiana may meet these people in the future? I know you don't live for others' approval—but for heaven's sake, Darcy. You're not above the world. I've always thought you a model, but that is not the behavior of a gentleman."

They'd reached the club, and one of the servers employed at White's opened the door for them.

Darcy looked at Bingley and a strange expression crossed his face. "Go ahead and eat. I'll—I'll wait on you this evening to discuss our plans."

He turned smartly and walked on, leaving Bingley gaping behind him.

"Sir?" the footman said.

Bingley took off his greatcoat and gave it to the waiting footman. Perhaps he had been too harsh? But when he thought of Miss Elizabeth—and Jane!—being duped by Wickham's falsehoods, perhaps to their own detriment, it made him angry. Darcy's indifference to it all was inexcusable.

Someone ought to tell Miss Elizabeth—and Jane!— the true story. And if it wasn't going to be Darcy, it was definitely going to be him.

And Jane... perhaps she didn't particularly fancy him, not the way he had thought, but he could not stop thinking about her. If Darcy was wrong about this—and he was—what else had he been wrong about?

CAROLINE POUNCED ON BINGLEY when he came home after dinner.

"Charles, we are both being idiots," she said, in the tone she often used when they were children, and she wanted him not to tattle to their mother. "I will merely write Lizzy a letter explaining that they are deceived. I wouldn't have dreamed of starting a correspondence on such a slight acquaintance, but since she has done so, it cannot be improper for me to reply."

"Or you could write to Jane about it, since you've been writing her."

Caroline made a face. "She's not a very good correspondent."

Bingley shrugged. "Nor am I, though surely the Bennets are more than acquaintances, wouldn't you say? We spoke with them weekly for months."

Caroline pressed her lips together in a sort of smile. "Certainly. I will write to the both of them, if you wish. There is no need for you to return there."

"Now that I've thought about it, however, I really think I ought to. It's irresponsible to lease a property and not look after it. I wonder Darcy did not tell me so. He should come by sometime tonight to discuss it. I'm not sure if he'll go back with me, but either way, I'm going." Charles paused on his way to the study, wondering at her wooden countenance. She really looked unhappy. "I know you have made plans to travel with Miss Elliot to Bath, and I would not interrupt your scheme for anything. You should still go."

He continued on his way, leaving Caroline making another strange noise, though he did not think she was choking.

AFTER LEAVING BINGLEY at the club, Darcy took a brisk evening walk through some of the lesser streets near Piccadilly. The ubiquitous smoke of London had been brought low by the cold and seemed to swirl around his ankles as he walked through the dark.

Bingley's words had caught him on the raw, and he found himself wondering what sort of person he truly was.

He didn't like introspection. Nor did he care for self-doubt. Unfortunately, he liked and respected Charles Bingley, and being taken to task by him was a novel and unpleasant experience.

Occasionally a friend held up a mirror that allowed you to see your blind spots—Darcy believed that was one of the benefits of friendship—and it would be hypocritical if he ignored what Bingley said.

Darcy went around to Manton's again and borrowed a pistol. With each shot, his mind turned over his behavior. Bingley's accusation of not acting like a gentleman rang in his ears along with the report of the gun.

Five wafers out of twenty.

When had Darcy's pride turned into indifference and arrogance? Was Bingley correct that Darcy thought himself above the world?

Eight wafers.

Had Darcy really forgotten that treating people as one wanted to be treated was vital to good breeding?

Thirteen.

He though further back, before Hertfordshire, before Ramsgate with Georgiana's fiasco. He got all the way to his childhood, remembering the lessons he learned from his father.

"A Darcy does the right thing," his father often said, or, "Don't judge your actions by others' approval. You're a Darcy, set your own standards."

Seventeen wafers.

His father had good intentions, but from childhood, Darcy had been taught that his name was synonymous with good behavior. His father taught him good morals and manners, but also that he was subject to no one's criticism.

When he finished the last wafer, Manton took the pistol. "You got eighteen out of twenty, Mr. Darcy, a fine display."

Mr. Darcy sighed. "That's the only thing I've done well today."

The lamps had been lit along the streets, and his town house in Berkeley Square had a welcome warm glow by the time he arrived back at his street, deflated but reconciled to himself. The work on the house was completed, so he had removed himself from the Bingley's town house yesterday.

Darcy had not eaten at the club after all, so he requested that the cook send up a pea soup and some of the ham from the previous day.

"Send it to the study, please," he told his butler.

His desk was an old-fashioned piece from the Stuart era, so heavy it had not been moved from this place for several generations. Darcy sat on the edge while looking through the post, and a letter with an ugly yellow wafer marked from Hertfordshire caught his eye.

He tore it open with one finger and read.

*Please excuse my forwardness in writing to you, sir, but I have inquiries to make about one George Wickham. He has run up some debts in my store, as well as several other establishments of Meryton. If you have any information on his habits and his likelihood of payment, particularly if he has committed crimes of monetary or other sort in another district, I would appreciate the information. I would not apply to you, except that Wickham has been quite free in using your name and asserting that you are familiar with his family and history. He has said some other things, but I don't give any heed to 'em—clearly he is insulting his betters, no matter what my wife says.*

*Again, please don't take my writing as an impertinence. My niece recommended it, and I thought it worth trying your patience.*

*Yours, etc.*

*J. Phillips*

Phillips? That was the name of the Bennets' relations in Meryton. The niece referenced would be Jane or Lizzy or one of their sisters.

He frowned.

Hard on the heels of the letter to Caroline, this seemed odd.

From Lizzy's letter to Caroline, it seemed Lizzy believed the slander about himself spread by Wickham. That had stung, even as he was telling Charles that it didn't matter what anyone believed.

Ugh, he *was* a hypocrite.

But then, this letter indicated she did *not* believe Wickham and had suggested that her uncle apply to him for information.

Which was it?

Perhaps Jane had advised her uncle to write him? But Darcy could not picture the eldest Miss Bennet, a simple, proper girl, to have prompted this note. The younger three Bennets were quite silly, and he didn't think their uncle would listen if they told him the price of eggs.

No, this letter spoke of Lizzy's influence, he was almost certain.

His butler, a very good fellow, came in with a tray and set it on the desk. "Quite dark, sir, I'll send Henry to light the fire and a few more candles."

"Yes, thank you."

"A wine for you this evening? White, perhaps?"

"Yes, perfect." Darcy went around to the chair for the desk, also a large oak affair, and pulled the tray towards him. The pea soup was warm and thick, and it made him think of Pemberley in February.

He looked again at the note. Lizzy was not foolish, and her uncle was most likely to listen to her.

So why the discrepancy? Did she believe Wickham in the right, which made Darcy feel rather ill, or did she not?

A slow smile crept over his face. He suspected a plot, and though he could not be sure exactly what it was, he admired her agency. If his suspicion was correct, the letter to Caroline had been a masterful little piece of manipulation.

*If* his suspicion was correct, Lizzy did not merely want Wickham dealt with—she wanted them all to return to Netherfield. Her hints to Caroline about staying away assured that.

But did she want Bingley back, or himself?

He wanted it to be him, but he had already been humbled today. If it was Bingley, was it on Jane's behalf? Darcy had certainly misread the entire situation, if that was so.

And somehow, without transgressing the bound of propriety at all, she had piqued Caroline's stubbornness, roused Charles to action, and engaged his sense of duty.

He looked at the letter and smiled. "Well done, Elizabeth, well done."

# { 13 }

WICKHAM GAVE MARY A NECKLACE in the shrubbery next to Lucas Lodge.

It was not such a nice little wilderness as they had at Longbourn, but there were hedges, winter-empty vegetable beds, and protected nooks that did not quite block the wind but did block the line of sight from the house.

Shaking off Anne Elliot had been a chore, but thankfully Musgrove had visited and taken her off somewhere. Musgrove seemed to feel that he was a brother or family member of the Elliots. He was always hanging about, and although he did not act particularly attracted to Mary, he had a proprietary way about him. In short, he was a nuisance, but at least today he'd proved useful.

Wickham suspected Musgrove meant to marry one of them. Mary might have been perfectly happy to accept, too, but Wickham fancied he had attached her enough that she considered herself in love with him now.

He knelt before her—stupidly cold grass under his knee—and removed the small gold trinket from his back coat pocket. He placed the small filigree heart in his hand, allowing the chain to dangle.

"My dear, I cannot give you palaces or mountain-tops, but please accept this small piece of my devotion." He blinked away imaginary emotion. "Then, wherever you go, I shall be able to picture a piece of our love around your neck."

Mary's neck was not particularly prepossessing. She was short and her neck was also. Her chest rose and fell, and her neck grew blotchy with white and red as she looked at the necklace. "Jewelry? It's so scandalous, I really ought not. Flowers, maybe..."

"Flowers are pretty for a day and die in the morning. I could never give you mere flowers."

She sank down on the bench in the embrasure, putting herself at his level. "Thank you, Wickham. It's so romantic."

Wickham stroked her chin, down to her clavicle, tracing around and back up to her ear. "You deserve this and more."

He had already undone the clasp of the necklace—little things like that were surprisingly important for not breaking the moment—and he now slid the necklace around her throat and took his time about latching it.

This put their faces very close together, and she looked deliciously thrilled.

Yes, the youngest daughter of a baronet would have to do for him. There was another heiress in the neighborhood, a Miss Mary King, but Wickham had already begun the game with this Mary. He couldn't very well switch now, not in the same limited society.

"Marry me," he said. "I know that I ought to ask your father, and I will. But he is far away, and I am worthless, and I cannot wait to hear your promise. Please, Mary?"

She gasped and held the necklace in her clenched hand. "A secret engagement?"

"Did you think me a cad? Merely flirting with you? I have never been more in earnest."

"I—I—Oh, yes, Wickham! I will marry you."

He kissed Mary then, and she did not shrink back at all.

Soon they were walking back toward Lucas Lodge, and Mary was still holding the heart. "What will I tell my sister? She'll know this is new."

"Tell her whatever you wish, even the truth. Surely she would be happy for you."

Mary scoffed. "You don't know her very well. Though, come to think of it, she *did* say she would support me if I chose you. As if her support would do anything much. She is such a strange one."

"I honor her for the sentiment in any case. Not many would counsel a beautiful young lady, the daughter of a baronet who could look as high as she wanted in the land, to accept a humble lieutenant like myself."

Mary squeezed his hand. "But I know you *ought* to have been a respectable member of the clergy, and I have not given up on that for you. I'm sure my father could give you the living attached to Kellynch. The very thing—for then I should be settled near my friends!"

He raised her hand to his lips and pressed his lips to it fervently. "Yes, the very thing."

Lizzy noticed the necklace, though Mary had tucked it into the collar of her pelisse by the time they all met up in the parlor at Lucas Lodge.

Mary kept touching it, sliding her finger along the chain.

Lizzy couldn't be certain, but she didn't think Mary had been wearing it when she arrived.

Lizzy was preoccupied by observing Mr. Musgrove and Charlotte as they played whist. Was it her imagination that he was more attentive than he had been?

Did he compliment Charlotte's first completed mitten with more sincerity than he did Anne's sonata on the pianoforte? Did he look up as happily when Lizzy entered the room as when Charlotte did?

The dratted man was far too good-natured. Everything pleased him, so it was difficult to tell what was special.

A man like Mr. Darcy now, a woman could tell where she stood with him. He did not smile at everyone who spoke to him or talk equally happily with every young lady.

Lizzy shook her head. She was a little distracted by the possibility of Mr. Darcy returning to Hertfordshire, and she was finding him in her thoughts more than she liked.

She forced herself to focus on her cards. She was paired with Charlotte's father, jovial Sir William, while Charlotte was paired with Mr. Musgrove.

Generally, Lizzy's younger sisters and the younger Lucas crowd would have insisted on something more lively, but Lydia, Kitty, Mary, and Jane were all laid up with a sick cold. For two days it had been nothing but coughing, sneezing, and complaints, and Lizzy had been relieved to go to Lucas Lodge for the evening.

Lizzy took the trick with a nine, and led with a three of hearts, hoping Sir William had a higher card of that suit.

"Ah, this trick is mine," said Mr. Musgrove, sitting to her left. "Ace of Hearts."

"A very good card." Sir William tossed down a five. "A fine card for a young man, though not quite as fine as the queen of hearts, I think you'd agree!" He chuckled at his joke. "Do you have a queen of hearts back in Hertfordshire, Musgrove?"

"No, no, I'm not married."

Charlotte examined her hand, her cards trembling slightly.

"Oh, I know," said Sir William. "But do you have a young lady? Anyone breaking her heart over you while you're away?"

"No one, unless you count my sisters, but I plan to return on Monday, so they cannot complain."

Charlotte finally withdrew a card and played a four of clubs. "Trump," she declared, collecting the trick.

"Ah, my daughter has stolen your highest heart! Ha, nothing for twenty-seven years and now she conquers two gentlemen in a month!"

He didn't mean anything by it, but Charlotte's face had gone quite red. "Mr. Musgrove and I are on the same team, Papa, so my trump is a waste. Only I could not play a heart in this round, for I am out."

Mr. Musgrove looked a little self-conscious as well. Lizzy would not have made such bold statements as Sir William, but it was enlightening. Musgrove ran a finger around his collar, as if it were too tight. "Now you lead off, Miss Lucas."

She led with a high trump, and Mr. Musgrove paid close attention to his cards.

Sir William sighed. "We shall lose, Miss Lizzy, unless you have better cards than you have played so far."

"I am not out yet," she assured him. Nor was she. If only Mr. Musgrove was staying a little longer!

It was about half an hour later—they'd won the game—when an interruption occurred.

The youngest Lucas boy—a lad of twelve—burst into the parlor and punched his brother in the arm. "John! I have just seen a phaeton going to Netherfield, and the finest pair of grays between the shafts—tandem style! They were beautiful."

John hit him in return, as a matter of course. "The gent at Netherfield left, and he didn't have a pair of gray carriage horses anyway."

"He must've bought them, for it was certainly him. He's got that orange hair; I know it was him. I bet Old Tim would let us help curry them. Let's go!"

John looked dubious. "Mr. Bingley probably brought his own groom. He won't use Old Tim."

"Yes, he will though, for there wasn't a groom up behind the gents."

John looked hopeful. He liked horses more than school, and they were old friends with the groom at

Netherfield. Before they could leave, Lizzy pulled them aside. "Was it both Mr. Bingley and Mr. Darcy?"

"Yes, Miss Lizzy—I think so," the boy said. "The other gentleman had a muffler so I couldn't see his face, but he was real tall."

Lizzy felt a surprising flutter at this news.

It was because her plan was working, she assured herself, not for any personal reasons. Speaking of plans... "John, I need a word with you, too."

BACK AT LONGBOURN that evening, their mother talked of nothing but Bingley's return.

Lizzy tried to comfort Jane through looks and silent sympathies.

Jane coughed and laid back against the couch, pulling a shawl closer around her. "We do not know his reasons, Mother. He may leave again soon."

Mrs. Bennet blew her nose and then sneezed. "Bingley *must* be back for good. I *knew* he would come. Oh, Jane! It is nothing to Mr. Collins." She sneezed again. "Bingley will save us all. We will live happily at Netherfield when your father has died, and Mr. Collins has turnt us out into the street. Lizzy, you are lucky that Jane has not your temperament. I'm sure she will not turn you away, though you *did* throw away our family prospects as if Longbourn was trash."

Corrie Garrett

Kitty and Lydia were both draped over the loveseat, flushed and miserable. "I don't even care that Bingley is back," Lydia moaned. "That is how sick I am."

Jane closed her own eyes, pressing a hand to her red forehead. "I would never turn Lizzy away—but that is not the point, Mama. We know nothing of Mr. Bingley's plans! He may only return for a few days. His sister wrote that he is not planning to settle here, and she wrote nothing of a visit. I don't think she wants to see me."

"Now, that is nonsense! I daresay she was just busy in London. Clearly Netherfield is the perfect situation for Bingley, whether she—*achoo!*—admits it or not. I have no great opinion of her understanding. She wore orange."

Caroline Bingley had probably never been dismissed so readily. It made Lizzy laugh, though she did sympathize with Jane's current discomfort. There *was* a possibility that Bingley would not renew his attentions to Jane. Time would have to tell.

Mary was the only one lying in her room, spending her misery alone, and her voice filtered down. "What are you all talking about? I suppose it is too much to ask that someone come talk to me."

Lizzy looked around at the draped bodies and rose. "I'm coming, Mary."

# { 14 }

DARCY DISCHARGED HIS DISTASTEFUL errands in the first two morning at Netherfield. He met with Mr. Phillips Friday morning, made a list of similar tradesmen who'd become lenders to Wickham, and visited them each in turn on Saturday.

He warned them of Wickham's past, though he left Georgiana out of it completely. He gave a brief outline of his involvement in Wickham's escapades and debt (both in Derbyshire and abroad), and trusted that the story would spread as needed among other tradesmen of Meryton.

He did not go so far as to pay Wickham's debts—not feeling that he owed it to either Wickham or the town—however, in warning them now, most seemed to feel that he had done enough. They would cut off his credit and could even contact his superior officer to garnish his wages if he did not begin to pay them down before the militia moved on.

This was all distasteful, but having begun, Darcy did things thoroughly.

On Saturday afternoon, he walked back toward Netherfield from Meryton. Now that the tiresome part of the business was over, he could admit that it was a relief to have made the truth known, at least in one small burgh.

And if once or twice he thought he saw Lizzy and her sister, only to be disappointed when he realized it was only a similar figure or bonnet that had deceived him, he was to be forgiven for the weakness. It had been a trying few days.

When he actually *did* come across Lizzy on the road that led along the Lea, he doffed his hat and bowed. She was not accompanied by her sisters or friends today, but merely with a maid who looked none-too-happy to be trudging to town on a damp December day.

She paused to acknowledge his bow with a slight curtsey and cheery, "Good day, Mr. Darcy. Welcome back to Meryton."

There was a laughing twinkle in her eye, but she said nothing else. Would she really go on without even a proper acknowledgement? It was *her* doing that Bingley was back at Netherfield at all.

"A fine day, Miss Elizabeth, are your sisters well?"

She paused. "No! Sadly, they all have a terrible cold. Jane and Lydia are on the mend, though Kitty and

Mary and my mother are still poorly. I'm on my way to the apothecary."

"You are lucky to have escaped the illness."

"Yes, though if you saw the quantity of blankets, tea, gruel, and handkerchiefs I have fetched and carried this past week, you'd forgive me for not feeling my luck excessively. Health is wasted on the healthy; it is only the sick who want it."

He smiled. "You have put me in mind of an errand. I'll turn back with you."

If his joining her was too abrupt, she did not show it. The maid sniffed and walked behind them.

"I am sorry to hear about your family's indisposition. You have put your time to good use, however."

She narrowed her eyes, unsure of his meaning. "I suppose. I have read a great deal."

"And written?"

Her lips twitched. "I don't know what you mean. Did Miss Bingley accompany her brother again to Netherfield? Local gossip has sadly failed me. If she has, I apologize for our negligence in failing to call on her. The sickness in the house has kept us at home."

"She is not there. She accompanied Miss Elliot and Sir Walter Elliot to Bath."

"Ah. I did hear from Anne that that was possible."

"You thought your letter would change Caroline's plans?"

Lizzy took a longer glance at him. "I take it you saw the letter?"

"I heard the gist of it from Bingley. You are hiding your disgust at my character flaws most adeptly. I honor your restraint."

Behind them, Alice gasped and tried to cover it with a cough.

Lizzy flushed but also laughed. "You need not walk on our heels, Alice. And you, Mr. Darcy—It is most provoking in you to always guess correctly! You are right that I may have warned Miss Bingley a bit more strongly than I felt, though the rumors are very real. I was glad to hear that you and Mr. Bingley have come back. I spoke with my uncle yesterday evening, and he told me what you planned to do, what you said."

Darcy nodded. "I don't particularly want to discuss it further," he glanced significantly at the maid trailing them, "but if you need further proof of Wickham's duplicity, I can provide it."

"Thank you." She came to a stop in front of the apothecary shop. "And now I think I ought not keep you any longer, for you were going the other direction."

Darcy knew he ought to walk away. Instead, he held the door for her. "After you. Somehow Wickham has not racked up debt here, so I have not happened to visit the apothecary."

"What an oversight!"

Darcy smiled but allowed her to go to the counter and make her requests. Darcy found the shop to be similar to the one in Lambton, the town near Pemberley. As a boy, he had sometimes gone there to buy candy. The apothecary could reliably be called on to carry not just remedies, but perfumes, spices, and confections.

Why had he prolonged his visit by entering with her? What was this madness that overtook him whenever she was nearby? At least during his first stay in Hertfordshire, he'd kept a tolerable coldness toward her. Now his self-control and feigned indifference were deserting him.

At her turn, Lizzy requested peppermint water, Epsom salt, and laudanum, which last item was hopefully for her mother and not her sisters.

While he waited, Darcy spied a shelf with bags of licorice, boxes of lemon drops, and wrapped bars of marzipan and nuts. There really was nothing like the confections at a good apothecary. Perhaps for Georgiana...

Lizzy joined him with her cloth bag hanging from her shoulder. She was still bemused that he was voluntarily waiting for her. She'd thought her letter to Caroline would make him stiffer and more standoffish, not less.

Alice looked at her with wide eyes when Mr. Darcy's back was turned. Lizzy gave her a reproving glare.

He hefted a box of lemon drops, and then set it back on the shelf.

"I wouldn't think a sweet tooth in keeping with your views on self-control," Lizzy said.

"It isn't, though I like licorice. I was thinking of my sister." He went back to the door to the street, pulling it open for her. "But the postage to mail Georgiana sweets from Hertfordshire would be ridiculous."

"That sounds more like you."

"I'll order some from the shop in Lambton for her. Then they'll be fresh."

The breeze had picked up, and Lizzy pressed a hand to her bonnet as they went back down the street.

"May I carry the bag for you?" he asked.

"Oh, it's not that heavy." The pound of Epsom salt was a little awkward, but not terrible. Alice walked behind them again, and Lizzy wondered what tale she would tell at Longbourn of this encounter with Mr. Darcy.

Oddly, Lizzy was enjoying herself and had no desire to get rid of him. "Forgive me if I overstep, but you seem quite cheerful considering the news that brought you back."

"There is always satisfaction with completing an onerous task."

"True. Will you and Mr. Bingley return to London this week?" They were leaving the town again, back on the path toward the stream and Longbourn.

"Not quite yet, no. Bingley is—well, I'm sure he'll not wish to leave before waiting on your family." He glanced back at Alice, who was all but dogging their steps again to eavesdrop.

Lizzy raised her brows in exasperation, and Alice fell back to a more discreet distance.

Darcy continued. "Since it has been forcibly indicated to me that I think myself 'above the world,' I wished to ask you something. It will come as no surprise to you that my friend Bingley is enamored with your sister. I did not, on our previous visit, believe that she reciprocated. However, I may have overstepped, and I wished to find out—before more pressure is put on her—whether I was correct."

Lizzy untangled this for a moment. She couldn't help saying, "That is the most upright request for gossip I have ever heard."

Darcy grew stiff, and the lines between his brows formed again. "My motives, however, are quite different."

"Yes, that wasn't fair of me." Clearly he was not used to being teased, even gently. Lizzy smiled to herself. "Thank you for asking. I can assure you that Jane thinks very highly of Mr. Bingley. I can't speak for her... but I suspect his regard is *fully* reciprocated."

"That is what I wished to know." He sighed. "Perhaps I only hoped for her indifference, and thus blinded myself. I abhor it when people allow their prejudice to blind their intellect."

"To be fair, my sister is shy and not at all dramatic. She feels deeply but does not wear her heart on her sleeve." Lizzy hesitated. She wanted to ask why he didn't want it to be true, but she knew the answer, didn't she? Their lack of wealth and status.

Perhaps she curled her lip as these thoughts passed through her mind. He seemed to guess.

"You are sensible young woman. You can't expect a man to *rejoice* in such connections."

Lizzy suspected she knew the crux of his disgust, for she had heard Miss Bingley whisper to him about their "uncle in Cheapside."

"You have not met my Uncle Gardiner, so you can hardly judge him merely because he lives in Cheapside. He and my aunt are truly intelligent and refined people. I am proud to have such connections."

It was Mr. Darcy's turn to look taken aback. "I was not referring to your uncle; I was referring to your family. If their behavior at Bingley's ball was typical, well, Bingley would be gaining a silly, immature, and occasionally, wild set of sisters." He compressed his mouth. "I'm sorry. I know your sisters are young, which is some excuse, but the lack of discipline and consistency by your parents is almost worse than their behavior."

"I suppose you have extremely high standards for an accomplished *family* as well as the accomplished woman Miss Bingley spoke of. Were my family deficits enough to convince you that Jane was indifferent to Mr. Bingley?"

"You're angry, but you already agreed that your elder sister's serenity is not easy to interpret. I can add that neither you nor she share in any part of my criticism; you both remained above reproach on all occasions."

This took some of the sting out of his words, and his further apology helped.

"I am sorry to give you pain," he added, "but since you guessed that I had removed Bingley, I felt you were owed some explanation."

"I did not guess it. I assumed it was Miss Bingley. But thank you—I suppose—for your honesty."

They were interrupted by two gentlemen on horseback, Mr. Bingley and Mr. Musgrove.

"Hullo, Darcy!" Bingley called. "Look who I've run into. It's Muskie, my friend from Cambridge. He says he's committed to hunting with a friend later, but I stole him away for a bit. We got up to such fun and gigs back then."

Lizzy greeted the men with smiles. "Don't let me detain you. I really must bring my things home."

Mr. Darcy turned aside to her. "May I carry your bag the last half-mile? It looks heavier than you admit."

"Nonsense. I've already taken too much of your time. Good day, Mr. Darcy."

He looked disappointed, and for a moment she thought he'd press it. Instead he nodded and turned to talk to his friends. They walked on, the sound of the hoofs receding behind her. Mr. Darcy soon left them and cut diagonally across the field toward a stile that would allow him to take a shortcut to Netherfield.

Lizzy felt an unexpected heaviness in her throat as she headed home. This made her laugh, for it was utterly ridiculous that she would feel any tenderness toward Mr. Darcy that might be injured by his disdain for her family. He had been trenchant, but were his words really worse than what she had said more than once to Lydia—particularly on finding her in another officer's embrace?

Stupid man, for making her care what he thought!

He liked her, she was sure of it now. He had unbent more in this conversation than in the previous eight weeks of their acquaintance. But he had no serious intentions toward her, that was clear. He might allow

Bingley to return to Jane—that lifted Lizzy's spirits—but he would never "lower" himself to their level.

And did she want him to?

Stupid *Lizzy*.

She kicked a clod of cold dirt, and it flew and broke apart on the path. "I am an idiot, Alice."

Alice had closed the distance between them. She shook her head. "I don't know how you talked to him for so long, miss. He glares and I can't remember my name, let alone where I'm steppin'. Do you think he's not so bad as people say?"

"No, he's not," Lizzy said. Not that that helped her very much. "Mr. Wickham has very much to answer for."

Alice giggled. "Wickham is so handsome, though."

Lizzy grimaced. "He is. There is some great mis-management with those gentlemen. One has all the ap-pearance of good without the substance, and the other the substance without the manner."

Alice frowned over this. "I don't know, but Mr. Darcy looked quite friendly today." She giggled. "A fine conquest, Miss Lizzy."

"Hush, Alice. He was speaking to me of Jane's cor-respondence with his sister."

Alice did hush her tongue, but apparently not for long. Only an hour later, when the sun was halfway toward the horizon of cold hills and fallow fields, Lizzy's mother screamed.

It was one of her happy outbursts, and Lizzy's name quickly followed. "Lizzy! Oh! Where are you? Where is she, Hill?"

Lizzy sat with a book by the hearth in her father's library.

He raised his eyebrows at her. "Murdered someone?"

Lizzy laughed, "I don't think so."

Her mother heard her. "Lizzy? There you are, hiding in your father's library. Hill tells me that Mr. Darcy spent an *hour* in town with you today! No, my dear Mr. Bennet, *you* can leave if I am distracting you, for I really must speak to Lizzy."

Lizzy resignedly closed her book, stroking its purple velvet cover wistfully.

Mrs. Bennet put her hands on her hips. "Can this be true? Mr. Darcy is such a disagreeable man that you have my pity." She allowed a brief moment of silence for her pity to fill the room, then rushed on. "But at the same time, he is worth *ten* thousand a year! Hill says that Alice says he flirted with you."

Mr. Bennet raised his spectacles from where they'd slid down his nose. "My dear wife, surely you do not believe the servants' gossip? Unless, Lizzy, you *were* flirting with him, in which case I beg you to tell your mother all about it. In another room."

"I was not. Alice is a great storyteller, with an active imagination."

Mrs. Bennet shook her head at Lizzy. "Yes, she is, but I have also heard from my brother Philips that you all but *wrote* the letter that brought Mr. Darcy and Bingley back into the neighborhood! Oh, Lizzy, you are such a *clever* girl, and I am glad it is not for nothing, as I have long feared! What a triumph, to bring them both back, and to have Mr. Darcy showing you attention! Why, there is nothing like it. And you were so sly, you said nothing!"

Lizzy's father arched an eyebrow. "You have been industrious, Lizzy. Please tell me you have not also bewitched Mr. Collins into a return?"

"I earnestly hope not."

Mrs. Bennet squeezed Lizzy's hands. "Ten thousand pounds a year!"

"Mr. Darcy spoke to me of Mr. Bingley *only*. You must not make a molehill into a mountain."

"And," Mr. Bennet added, "you have miraculously cured your mother's cold, Lizzy. You have unplumbed depths."

"I'm sure it is no wonder I should feel better, with this news!" said Mrs. Bennet. "I was already determined Jane should be well, and you see she is doing much better today. Now that I have the peppermint water, I shall be just the thing. We simply *must* call on them tomorrow."

"On Sunday?" Mr. Bennet asked mildly. "I'm sure they would not mind, however irregular a call after church may be."

"Oh—well, perhaps I'll invite them for Sunday supper! That is unexceptionable. I'll have Jane write a note to Miss Bingley."

Lizzy grimaced. "I forgot to tell you, Mother, but Mr. Darcy says she did not accompany them. She is visiting friends in Bath."

"Oh? That is very strange and unnecessary. How is Mr. Bingley to have Jane to the house without a hostess? I do not like that at all. December is an absurd time of year to visit Bath."

"As ever, I am in total agreement with you, my dear wife," Mr. Bennet said.

"Yes, are we not always?" Mrs. Bennet trailed away, probably to rouse Hill and plan a Sunday supper for the gentlemen.

Mr. Bennet leaned over to take Lizzy's purple book, running it through his fingers thoughtfully. "What is this scheme, Lizzy? You have done something. Is it for Jane?"

"Partially."

"Ah. Matchmaking is a perilous art, besides being physically taxing. I wish you joy of your new hobby."

"It is not a hobby, at least, not for long. More of an effort at righting a wrong." She explained the business with Wickham and her uncle. "So you see, it was two birds with one stone. Or perhaps two birds with two stones, but you understand me."

"Perhaps you ought not to go into law, but yes, I do." He handed back her book. "I hope you are not in over your head."

# { 15 }

CAROLINE BINGLEY WAS NOT IN OVER her head, settled at Bath with Miss Elliot, but she could admit that the Elliots were not the easiest family to live with.

There could even, she imagined, be another side to their constant accusations that Anne was harsh and moody with them. They were a bit capricious and more than normally self-centered.

Caroline was benefitting from it, however, and she was too clearheaded to criticize.

She currently wore the softest shawl. It was on loan from Miss Elliot, for it matched Caroline's dress for the evening. It was cream-colored with a lavender paisley pattern that perfectly coordinated between her warm-toned blonde hair and her lavender evening gown.

She stroked the shawl while looking out the window towards the majestic curve of town houses. The Elliots' rented rooms were on Camden Crescent, one of the best and most desired residential streets in Bath. Camden Place was one of the seven "crescents" of Bath, a great row of three-story town houses in a graceful and striking curve. The Royal Circus was the most famous, perhaps—anyone who was *anyone* walked the Circus in mild weather—but Upper Camden Place was a fine situation, and it was only a few blocks to the Bath Assembly Rooms, or Upper Rooms.

She ran her fingers over the beautiful fabric of the shawl and made plans to purchase her own. It was not as if she could not afford it, as Miss Elliot had implied; this particular style of cashmere had simply not come Caroline's way before.

Miss Elliot sat near the other window in the rented town house, also looking out. "It is so dreary to have rain, and the umbrellas and hats block peoples' faces! How can I see if an acquaintance passes by?"

It was nearly six in the evening, quite dark, and soon they would leave for the concert.

Sir Walter stood in front of his mirror and adjusted his cravat. "What is worse, my dear, is that the rain steams up the windows and prevents anyone from looking *in* to see you or me. I daresay our acquaintances would keep their eyes open, knowing we are at Bath, but it does them no good in this weather. That must be why we have received so few cards."

Caroline stifled a snort. "But surely—I mean, you cannot expect your friends to look in every window for you."

He raised his eyebrows.

Caroline realized she had erred. "I'm sure if they *should* see Miss Elliot or yourself, they would leave a card. Your friends haven't yet realized their luck in having you at Bath."

"Indeed, they haven't. Now, that is a pleasant thought; it is like a surprise."

"You and Miss Elliot will light up the dreary month of December for them. As you have done for me."

"How nicely put," Sir Walter said. "Isn't that nicely put, Elizabeth?"

"Are you ready to go?" Miss Elliot said. "I see the carriage coming up the street now."

"Yes, my dear, but one mustn't rush. I don't know about the powder of this wig... it does not look perfectly set, and I hate when men's powder is dusted on their noses and chins instead of staying where it ought."

"I think you are over-cautious, Sir Walter," said Caroline. "I can't see even a speck."

"Perhaps, perhaps. I hold it is better to be over-cautious than under, however. So many men are utterly careless of the details! Even men who might, with the appropriate care, have nothing to be ashamed of in their appearance. It is really rare that good height, looks, breeding, and fashion are encompassed in one gentleman. Even Mr. Darcy, whom I know you fancied, Elizabeth, was not quite what I like in fashion. His clothes were a bit simple, a little dark, a little too austere."

Caroline adjusted her paisley shawl with care and averted her face. She really could not talk about Mr. Darcy with Sir Walter and Miss Elliot.

Sir Walter offered her his left arm, while Miss Elliot was on his right. "This is something like," he said. "Two lovely ladies on my arms, who are not badly shone off by me as their squire, even if I am older."

Their progress down the stairs, three abreast, was awkward, so his stately purpose was interrupted.

As Caroline fell back two steps behind them, Sir Walter apologized. "Poor Miss Bingley, we take ill care of you."

"Not at all. I learnt to navigate stairs years ago, if you can believe it."

He chortled at this.

Caroline had a growing suspicion that if she wished it, she could become the next Lady Elliot. To marry a wealthy baronet was everything her mother could have wished for her. It was everything Caroline could wish for herself.

Sir Walter *was* older and rather vain, even by Caroline's standards, but she did not mind him. Nor did she mind the need for flattery to keep him in good spirits.

Still, she was uncertain. He was no Mr. Darcy.

Sir Walter was affable—if one was beautiful—and he was considerate—if he thought of it, and it cost nothing. There were far worse gentlemen out there, and he showed a distinct willingness to be won by a pretty woman.

Perhaps it soothed his vanity to think he could attract a woman thirty years his junior. When Caroline offered slight flattery, he reacted always with appreciation, and she thought he would easily be led on to a proposal.

But... she hesitated. She was younger than Miss Elliot. Would Miss Elliot be angry?

Would Caroline care once she was established as the mistress of Kellynch Hall?

These were all very interesting questions.

Their footman held an umbrella and escorted each member of the party individually to the waiting carriage. The puddles on the even paving stones of Bath were slight, and with careful stepping, Caroline could avoid them.

Sir Walter and Miss Elliot already sat in the forward-facing seat.

Miss Bingley took the rear-facing seat with a tight smile. She was not accustomed to being the lesser in a relationship, but sometimes needs must.

As Lady Elliot, she would command respect.

But would she be happy?

She would have status and wealth. Perhaps that would be enough.

And how *shocked* Mr. Darcy would be to hear the news.

MR. MUSGROVE STOOD QUIETLY in the under-
growth near the lake, his shotgun in hand.
The ducks had forsaken the water when
he and John Lucas arrived, but they decided to wait for
them to return.

"Nothing like a Saturday of shooting," John said.
"I'd much rather do this than Latin and mathematics."

"I agree ," Mr. Musgrove said. "I've forgotten all the
Latin from school; I was a dunce at it, but I can tell you
the finer points of Manton's new hunting piece. If
they'd taught that sort of thing at school, I would have
done much better."

"Have you been to Manton's? My father says he will
take me up to London and let me shoot there, but he
hasn't yet."

"Yes, I have. Most competent fellow, dead good shot,
and brilliant with weapons."

The gray of the lake was broken with ripples, as if a comb had been dragged across it. The water reflected the sun in coin-size patches. The clouds were also gray, though occasionally blue sky poked through, allowing a shaft of sunshine to warm the landscape.

"Sounds bang-up," John breathed. "I can't wait to shoot there."

John Lucas was a stocky, dark-headed young fellow of sixteen. He was a good lad and already a good shot. Mr. Musgrove liked him far more than he did his own brother Richard. Richard didn't like shooting and was too lazy to even sit near a lake and wait for a goose. On the few occasions when Mr. Musgrove had badgered his younger brother into coming, Richard had been loud enough to scare the birds, never stopped complaining, and (somehow) got drunk enough to vomit two hours into the outing.

"I hear the ducks," John breathed now. "Flying from the west, I think."

Musgrove couldn't hear them, but he believed his young friend. Slowly, he swung his shotgun to a more ready position. He didn't cock it against his shoulder yet, for it was too heavy to hold there for long.

John's bird dog, a mongrel of gray and white with a wiry coat and an Irish wolf-hound look to him, waited patiently at his master's feet.

The birds descended without much warning from the low clouds. Both the men swung their shotguns to their shoulders in one smooth motion. They'd loaded earlier, packing the shot and powder, and now both guns barked at almost the exact same moment. One report sounded like the echo of the other.

"Two hit!" John cried. "Very nice. Go, Titan!"

The dog took off into the scrub bushes and gorse, and soon could be seen circling west around the lake, nose flared as he raced to fetch the downed birds.

The other ducks had scarpered off with the loud shots, but John assured him he could still get good sport with grouse or partridge for the next hour.

"Certainly," Mr. Musgrove said. "Perhaps someday you might come shoot with me at Uppercross. Excellent deer stalking in December."

"Oh, I would like that, thank you, sir." John whistled for his dog, and soon Titan was trotting back, a limp duck held respectfully in his soft mouth. "You go back this week?" John asked.

"Yes. Tomorrow's church, and I'll pay a few more goodbye visits. Monday morning I'll be on my way. I'm escorting Anne and Mary Elliot to Bath to join their father."

"Oh, yes, they're your neighbors." John had not much interest in them, though he would be glad to have them out of his house. He plucked the duck from his dog, working towards saying something tricky. He folded the duck's wings in and tucked it into his game bag.

He sent Titan back to fetch the other duck.

Miss Lizzy's request was not quite as easy as John had expected. He sucked on a sore tooth.

John liked his sister Charlotte—she was bully good for a girl—but he wasn't at all sure Musgrove would want her. There wasn't much exciting about one's sisters.

Still, John had promised Lizzy to mention a few things, and he would do it. Lizzy was not as pretty as Jane, but full of laughter. John may have had a few daydreams about Lizzy, and when she said she could "depend on his help and discretion," he wanted to oblige.

"I—er—I think Charlotte will miss you." John immediately bit his cheek. What a dunce he was! "We all will. Go on, Titan," he yelled at the dog. "You've not got the other duck yet, old boy."

"It's been pleasant to reconnect with my cousins, though I'm ready to go home for the holiday."

"Yes." John sucked his teeth. "We'll have a wedding in a couple weeks. Going to mess up Christmastime."

"Ah, yes... Mr. Collins and your eldest sister. Your mother told me."

"Mama's pleased as punch because Collins is to inherit Longbourn. The rest of us though... we don't like him."

"Well, it's natural a boy might not like his sister's intended. You've had her to yourselves for a long time."

"It's not *that*," John said, a little offended. "I'd be happy for Charlotte to hie off somewhere else, as we're crowded enough, but Mr. Collins—eh, he's a clunch. One of those sorts who thinks he's better than everybody but pretends to be so *grateful* and humble. He's happy enough to marry Charlotte, but the things he says! He told her he'd 'never talk about how she's older and *plain* and not to worry!' I took offense and I'm not even a *female*."

John nodded to himself. Now he'd done what Miss Lizzy asked.

Mr. Musgrove was frowning as John's dog brought the second duck back. This one was wet, and John shook it off before putting it in his game bag.

Lizzy had said, "Don't get creative, John, just a few bits about why you don't like him. Remember—you'll all miss Mr. Musgrove; you all hate Mr. Collins."

Mr. Musgrove offered John a linen to clean his hands. "I suppose any boy of sixteen would find a clergyman rather dull and... uncongenial."

"Aye, but Mr. Collins is awful, everybody agrees. He only offered for Charlotte to save face when Miss Lizzy said no."

"What? Surely he didn't tell her so."

"I don't know what he told Charlotte, but he don't ever stop talking, so he might've. He was mighty eager to rub it in at Longbourn."

Mr. Musgrove frowned even more. "That does sound unkind, but we probably ought not gossip about him."

"Alrighty."

John felt the satisfaction of a job well-done, and led Mr. Musgrove uphill, in the direction of a likely copse of pines for partridge.

CHARLOTTE WAS AWARE that her wedding was in two weeks, but she was trying not to think of it, even as she embroidered handkerchiefs with WC for William Collins.

Anne was in the schoolroom, playing their pianoforte, and Mary Elliot had fallen asleep on the divan nearby.

Charlotte's stitches were neat, and the design of deep green leaves and vines flowed in efficient fashion around the edge of the white cloth as she worked. She used a small sewing hoop to keep the fabric taut, and as she stuck the sharp needle repeatedly through it, her mind felt equally pierced.

Unbidden, a letter was composing itself in her mind.

*Dear Mr. Collins,*

*You have done me a great honor, but I regret that I have made a mistake. I'm afraid I must withdraw from our engagement. I deeply apologize for disappointing you and drawing back from this agreement. Please accept my heartfelt thanks for the honor of your proposal...*

But no. She jabbed the needled into the cloth and pulled it through. That was ridiculous. She could not cry off from the *one* chance at matrimony she'd had in her long days as a spinster. She was nearly twenty-eight! How many women got a good offer at twenty-eight?

She would embroider these benighted handkerchiefs and work on her modest trousseau and count her blessings.

Still, that letter would obtrude.

*Dear Mr. Collins,*

*I've contracted a terrible sickness and am not expected to live out the year.*

No.

*Dear Mr. Collins,*

*I've found that my affections are engaged elsewhere—*

"Ow!" Charlotte cried. Her thumb welled up with blood, for she had stuck the needle well into the pad.

Mary only snorted in her sleep and sank deeper into the cushion.

Charlotte sucked the blood off. She found a spare scrap of wool in the sewing basket to press to the spot.

"Oh, dear," her mother whispered. "Do try not to be clumsy. I don't have any spares for you to embroider."

"I know, I didn't get any blood on it."

"Thank heaven for small blessings." She looked out the window. "There's John and Mr. Musgrove coming down the hill. I like him excessively. Exactly the kind of man I'd like John to be. I wish your sister Anna were a little older; she would be just the thing for him."

Charlotte pressed viciously against the wool on her thumb. "You sound like Mrs. Bennet."

"Well, no wonder, we've both a lot of children to see provided for. Longbourn! I can hardly believe you'll be mistress there someday. It's such a comfort to have you well-settled."

"It is hard on the Bennets."

"Oh, pooh. She'll see Jane married to Bingley yet; they'll be perfectly fine."

Charlotte and her mother both heard the rear door of the house open, and the men's steps were loud and then quiet as they removed their muddy boots and took their kill to the kitchen. It would be the job of the cook to dig the buckshot out of the bird.

Soon they entered the parlor, both in their stockinged feet. Mr. Musgrove no longer stood on ceremony with them, as he had visited almost daily either to shoot with John or to see Anne and Mary, who were staying with them.

The creaking of the door and the cold from the hall woke Mary from her Saturday afternoon slumber. She pushed herself upright and rubbed her eyes. "Lord, I am so sleepy. Are you back already?"

Mr. Musgrove retrieved his indoor shoes, sensible brown pumps with no heel, which he had left near the fire. "Yes, are you rested, I hope?"

John got his slippers, which were also warming there.

"Yes, I suppose." Mary rubbed her eyes again and played with the small necklace she wore with her blue muslin day dress. "You know, I don't want to go to Bath just now. I think you should take Anne back, and I'll stay until Father is back home."

Charlotte and her mother avoided eye contact. They would never turn their wealthy friends away, but both Charlotte and her mother would be glad to be rid of Mary.

"We don't want to overstay our welcome," Mr. Musgrove reminded her. "And your father made plans. I'm bound to carry them out."

Mary made a petulant face and slid the pendant back and forth on the chain again. "He doesn't care. He and Elizabeth are so selfish. They never care what *I* want to do. And before you say it, neither does Anne! She just wants to keep everything the *same*."

Mr. Musgrove quirked an eyebrow. "Still, I think we must keep to our plans, Mary."

Charlotte had reached the end of her thread, so she tied a knot and snipped the end with her scissors.

"What have you there?" Mr. Musgrove asked.

"Just a handkerchief." She passed the hoop into his outstretched hand.

"Oh. Of course, for Mr. Collins."

"Yes."

He passed it back at once, nearly dropping it. His hand grazed Charlotte's, and her eyes went to his. For a moment, they both stared at one another. Then he rose. "I'd best get back to the Longs. They're expecting you all for dinner, don't forget."

Mary perked up her head. "Did your aunt invite any of the officers?"

"Yes, I believe so, most of the normal party."

She smiled. "Excellent."

# { 17 }

WICKHAM ALMOST DIDN'T GO TO the Long's dinner party that evening. It'd been a trying day at best, catastrophic at worst.

What the devil did Darcy mean by coming back and spreading his ill-humor over the neighborhood? Wickham had been accosted by no less than three tradesmen and two gambling cronies. It'd been the same variation all day.

"No more credit here."

"Not likely, Lieutenant, let's see some payment on your tab."

"Ha, on credit? That game won't fly anymore, Wickham."

There was Mr. Phillips first, then the pub owner where the officers often drank. Last, and worst, had been a hostel owner Wickham didn't even know well, but had lost to at cards only a fortnight ago.

"Debt of honor," the man had said, "I trust you'll be good for it?"

"I'm offended you would ask."

"Not accusing you of anythin', but I heard some rumors and wanted to check."

"I am good for it."

Wickham stewed in the small room provided to him as a junior officer at the lodging in town. He'd gotten the lay of the land from Mr. Phillips, and it was no good.

Darcy was so prejudiced against him, he colored their entire history as if *Wickham* had been at fault. What rot! When it was Darcy's resentment and greed that were the foundation of all Wickham's problems!

If Darcy turned the town of Meryton against Wickham, and with them Wickham's superior officers, there would be nothing for it but flight. It wasn't so good to desert from His Majesty's army, but how was Wickham to live under prejudice and oppression?

Wickham decided to attend the Longs' dinner when he found out that Mr. Darcy was not planning to attend. Free food was always worth something, and Mary Elliot must be inoculated against the rumors.

She smiled at him across the room when he arrived with Captain Denny and Colonel Forster and the other officers. Denny didn't seem to have heard anything yet, though Colonel Forster was a little cooler than usual.

Mary raised the pendant he'd given her and pressed it to her lips, perhaps in a way that she thought was seductive. It might have been, if he hadn't been anxious and angry.

Wickham made the rounds of the room both to learn the current gossip and to deflect from his interest in Mary. He might still sabotage his own game if he was not cautious.

Mrs. Bennet smiled at him vaguely, but she was distracted with Lady Lucas.

"I tell you, he has shown quite a preference for Lizzy!" Mrs. Bennet said. "It would be beyond anything. And, of course, Bingley is back! Oh, I am so happy, I can only wish you were as well. Mr. Collins—though very correct—is nothing to them."

Lady Lucas cleared her throat. "To be sure, however, a bird in the hand is worth two in the bush, as they say."

"Who says? I do not like birds in my bushes. They eat all the berries. It is no wonder you harvested so few blackberries last year, if you encourage birds in the vines."

Wickham moved on.

Mrs. Long, the hostess of the evening, swatted his arm and flirted with him and Denny.

Finally, Wickham made it to the Elliot sisters. Mary was half-reclined on a couch, one foot tucked under. Anne stood behind her.

Wickham smiled, bowed, and brought Mary's hand up for a kiss. "Miss Mary, Miss Anne, pleased to see you both. I am devastated to hear you'll be leaving Hertfordshire."

Anne laid a hand on her sister's shoulder. "We must not trespass on the Lucases' kindness any longer."

Mary rolled her eyes. "They don't mind having us, you're just tired of being here. And it's not fair!"

"Mary, please. We're in company."

"All the more reason not to treat me like a child."

"Then please act like the mature young lady you are," Anne said.

Wickham attempted to look sympathetic and supportive, but he was distracted from the small spat by a feeling that someone was staring at him.

A quick glance found that it was Elizabeth Bennet. Her eyes were narrowed, as if she were weighing him in the balance and finding him wanting. Had Darcy spilled his lies to *her*? That seemed odd.

Darcy was standoffish and proud with strangers, especially with women, the idiot. Wickham could not imagine Darcy telling his woes to a member of the Bennet family.

The only way it would happen was if Darcy was interested in Elizabeth.

That filled Wickham with a sudden flicker of rage. Were Mrs. Bennet's ramblings about *Darcy*? Why should Darcy have the privilege to look wherever he chose for a wife, while Wickham had to try for a wealthy, spoiled, annoying girl?

Wickham liked Lizzy, and if he'd had half a chance, she would have liked him too.

"Wickham? Did you hear what I said? Would that not be pleasant?" Mary Elliot asked with an edge to her voice.

Wickham forced himself back to her. "I'm sorry, what was that?"

She huffed. "I could stay with the Lucases until my father returns from Bath."

"If I had only my own preferences to consider, you would stay forever. But I could never counsel you to inconvenience your father or sisters."

He smiled at Anne expressively. Skeptical lines appeared between her eyes. She looked as if she wanted to believe him but didn't. Wickham must be losing his touch. He gave Mary a significant, apologetic look and moved away.

After dinner, the ladies retired to Mrs. Long's parlor while Wickham and the other officers and gentlemen remained at the table. The butler brought out two bottles of port and a bowl of rum punch.

As the men relaxed, Wickham excused himself from the table. The other men barely noticed, and Wickham slipped into the hall.

He found Mary in the stairway embrasure, just as they had planned.

"Oh, Wickham!" She threw herself at him.

His arms went around her, and he kissed her, as a matter of course.

Mary turned her face away. "I cannot bear to leave! What if I should never see you again? No one cares what *I* want to do, you see how I am neglected."

"I am overcome at the thought of your departure," Wickham said. "Even more so as—well, I should not burden you."

"Burden me with what?"

"No, no. My trials are not your problem. You are an angel above all earthly things."

"What trials? Please tell me. I am stronger than people think, but everyone treats me like an invalid."

"It is only—perhaps you heard that Mr. Darcy and Mr. Bingley have returned to Netherfield?"

"Yes, though they did not call on me, which was rather rude."

"Mr. Darcy has been busy turning the people of Meryton against me. His resentment—I have told you of it before—has found a fresh outlet. Everywhere he tells people that I am a spendthrift and a rake. That I renege on debts and that no female is safe with me!" Wickham kissed Mary's hand fervently. "As if I have eyes for any woman but yourself."

"That's awful! Why must he pursue you so? You must tell people the truth."

"I have, and I will. But sadly, in our fallen world, those with money and resources are more believed than those without. I am thankful that you are not so blind."

"Of course not. I hope I know a true story when I hear one. But what about me? Are—are you breaking things off with me because of his slanderous stories?"

"Never," Wickham vowed. "In fact—though I shudder to ask it of one so pure—I have even contemplated elopement."

Mary's mouth opened in a perfect o.

"Tell me you understand. It is my desperation that makes me bold."

Mary bit her lip for real this time. "Do you mean we should go to Gretna Green? I hear it is very cold in Scotland, and I am prone to the most *vicious* coughs in the winter."

Wickham almost laughed. How helpful that Mary's hypochondriac tendencies would work in his favor. "Not Scotland, London. A special license."

"Oh! That sounds much better."

"It is not my first choice to wed you in such clandestine way, but if Darcy truly poisons the town against me, it may be the only path! We have already been under the stairs too long. Will you meet me secretly, Sunday afternoon? Half past three, in the copse of firs on the lane outside Lucas Lodge."

"I'll be there."

Wickham pressed his lips to her jaw, her neck, then slipped back to the dining room.

Charlotte rarely had more than a glass of wine at dinner, but tonight she allowed herself more.

She wanted to forget the future and the past and enjoy the present without that aching regret in her stomach. She wanted to enjoy the last night of Mr. Musgrove's visit.

Soon, with a pleasant warmth in her face, she was able to breathe freely again and to stop composing doomed letters to Mr. Collins.

"You look very nice tonight, Miss Lucas," Mr. Musgrove told her, when the gentlemen joined the ladies after dinner.

"Thank you." The advent of the men raised the noise level, and the officer's red coats made the room feel warmer than ever. She felt more relaxed than she had in weeks.

He sat down on the settee next to her and crossed his ankles. "Have you ever been to Somerset, Miss Lucas?"

"No, I haven't. I would like to visit someday."

"You'll be fixed in Kent, and that is not so far. Perhaps you and your husband will come visit."

"Yes, perhaps." Charlotte was careful not to say anything negative about Mr. Collins. She was not drunk, she was merely relaxed. "I don't know if he likes to travel. Do you like to travel, Mr. Musgrove?"

"Oh, not in the common way, to see mountains and great empty houses. I do like to visit my friends."

"Particularly for a good hunting season?"

He laughed. "Yes, exactly. I am very commonplace."

"I think you are very patient and humble."

"That's making me out to be quite a saint. Not at all, I assure you. If you'd ever seen me fishing you'd know I'm not so patient, nor so humble."

"Few fishermen are. Your mother must have trained you well, though."

"She's a good, comfortable soul, my mother. We're not much educated and not at all elegant, but you'll seldom find a happier family."

Charlotte smiled. She was sure he was right. He wasn't much educated, and he was, in his way, probably not much more intelligent than Mr. Collins. He was, however, kinder than Mr. Collins. He had an innate desire to see people happy and well that was entirely unselfish. He used his common sense for everyone's good.

"My mother just wants us all to be happy," he continued. "Of course, my brother Richard is a scamp, and her patience did him no good. What do you think is stronger, a boy's nature or the way he's raised?"

"I don't know."

"A friend told me about a scientific paper he'd read. The science chap said that intelligence and good behavior is all based on inheritance, our nature. Bad blood will out, and that sort of thing. Whereas 'nurture'—how someone is raised—is less important."

"I hope not." Charlotte thought of Mr. Collins. He was not very smart, though she did not care so much about that as about his vanity and pompous behavior. Would her children be the same as him? That made her less happy. "I hope it is some of both. One has only to look at a family to see that it cannot be all about nature. Even twins turn out so differently. On the other hand, it cannot be entirely how children are raised, or no one would ever excel more than their parents."

He laughed. "Good point. I haven't read the paper—science is not really in my line—but one must work with what one sees. I think there is a third component that science chap didn't even touch on."

"What is that?"

"Well, you've only to look at child in the grip of temptation to see a choice is made. Does he grab the sweetie from his sister, or stick his hands in his pockets? That's not necessarily what he was born with or what his mother taught him, it's his own choice. Adults are worse, for they learn to hide it. Children are more obvious."

"Do you want children? I suppose that is a stupid question; every man wants a son."

"I'll take any. I like my sisters, and I like my two youngest brothers. Sons would be useful on the farm, but we don't have any silly entailment to leave Uppercross away from the female line. If something happens to me and Richard, Louisa and her future husband would get the house, and my blessings on 'em both." He looked away. "I expected to get married this year, before Henrietta and Louisa are out, but that's one plan gone awry."

"I'm sorry." Charlotte felt warm all the way to her toes. "I've wanted to get married for years, so I know how that feels."

Lizzy held her cards loosely in her hand, for most of her attention was directed toward eavesdropping on Charlotte's conversation.

Charlotte was being quite forthright, even for her. Perhaps Charlotte and Mr. Musgrove did not need any more help after all.

"Lizzy, it's your play," said Mr. Long.

Lizzy looked at her cards again, but she could not focus or remember a single one. She played a low heart at random and tapped the other cards on the small wooden table, flicking restlessly at the corner of the table with her thumb nail.

Mrs. Long had set up a few whist tables, and Lizzy had gotten pulled into one, but her mind was preoccupied.

Lizzy had seen Mary Elliot slip away soon after the ladies separated after dinner, and she was willing to bet that Wickham had joined her. Should Lizzy tell someone? Anne Elliot, perhaps? Or Lady Lucas, who was Mary's host?

Then there was Charlotte. She was lovely tonight, the prettiest Lizzy had ever seen her. Charlotte was *not* plain (as Lizzy's mother and even Charlotte's mother often said), but she was not flashy. Lizzy liked her friend enormously. Tonight, Charlotte's cheeks were pink, and her eyes were bright. She was animated and happy.

But when she said, "I've wanted to get married for years, so I know how that feels," Lizzy's whole body winced.

That was so vulnerable, so unlike Charlotte! What was happening to her friend? Was she desperate? Had she decided to try for Mr. Musgrove? Lizzy wanted that, but she did *not* want it at the cost of her friend's dignity.

Lizzy feigned a cough, covering her mouth and hacking. Her eyes watered easily, and Mr. Long wrinkled his nose. "Bless you."

"I'm so sorry," Lizzy said. She cleared her throat with emphasis. "Anne, would you mind taking my place?"

Anne Elliot opened her eyes wide, but Lizzy didn't give her time to refuse. She coughed again and handed her cards to Anne. "Just a moment, I really must get some water."

Lizzy put her hand on Charlotte's shoulder. "Charlotte, could you walk with me a moment? I think the smoke from the tallows irritated my throat."

"Oh. Of course, Lizzy." Charlotte rose and swayed the tiniest bit.

Lizzy steadied her under the guise of using her for support. Was Charlotte *tossed*, as the saying went?

They went into the hall, which was cool, dim, and quiet.

Charlotte pressed a hand to her cheek. "I think I might have drunk too much of that wine that Colonel Forster brought."

Lizzy steadied her again. "That explains it. I heard Mr. Wickham say it was uncommonly strong. Do you feel ill?"

"No, not at all. I feel very well. Just a trifle dizzy." She smiled. "I like Mr. Musgrove."

"So do I." Lizzy had no idea what to do. They were not at Lucas Lodge, so she could not take Charlotte to her bedroom.

"You were right, Lizzy."

"Was I? I think we need some cold water. I'll drink some for my throat, and we'll put some on your face." Lizzy steered them toward the kitchen.

"You were right about Jane and Bingley. She didn't show him much affection, but he is back anyway. I'm very glad for her."

"Oh, that. Yes, I hope it will work out."

Charlotte stumbled against a narrow table in the hall and sent the Longs' post—a pile of envelopes and circulars with shiny wax seals in red, yellow, and purple—tumbling to the floor.

Lizzy bent to collect it.

"I still think marriage is a pragmatic undertaking," Charlotte said. The word pragmatic tripped her up for a moment. "Prag-ma-tic," she repeated. "Yes. But also you are right that it would be pleasant to marry someone I like and respect. I'm afraid I will be s-sentimental yet."

"Oh, Charlotte." Lizzy threw the post back on the table and led Charlotte the last few steps to the kitchen door, rimmed with warm light around the edges. The maids were still scrubbing from dinner, and the tea things had yet to be brought to the guests. That wouldn't happen for another hour or so.

"Excuse us," Lizzy said to the servants, who knew who she and Charlotte were quite well. "The smoke was bothering us."

There was a barrel of water in the corner by the door, from which the servants dipped out what was needed into basins, pitchers, or pots. Lizzy scooped out some water in the large iron ladle and took a sip. She'd agitated her throat while pretending to cough, a fitting punishment for subterfuge.

Charlotte stuck a finger in the water and made a face. "It is ice cold."

"Yes, it is just what we need. Get your face wet, my dear. It'll help."

Charlotte obediently wetted her hands and pressed them to her flushed cheeks. She gasped and grimaced.

"Once more," Lizzy said, guiding Charlotte's hands back. Lizzy splashed her own face too, rubbing her eyes and mumbling about smoke again—for the servants' sake.

"Oh, Lizzy, you wretch." After a few splashes, Charlotte used a linen towel to dry her face and hands and passed it to Lizzy.

"Much better," Lizzy said.

Back in the hall, dim and quiet, Charlotte sighed. "I was very forward with him, wasn't I? Oh—how embarrassing!"

"No, no, you don't need to be embarrassed. You were only friendly as yet, but I wanted to make sure you didn't say anything you'd regret."

Charlotte's cheeks were still red, so Lizzy couldn't tell if she flushed again.

Charlotte straightened the mail on the small table as they came back. "I told you not to judge me for choosing Mr. Collins, but you *must* be judging me now. And I deserve it. I'm an old maid and a fool."

"Never," Lizzy said. "Have you thought... perhaps a direct conversation with Mr. Musgrove?"

"More direct than *that*? And say what—that though I am four years older than him, have no fortune, and am engaged, he ought to marry me?" She shuddered.

"Perhaps not in those exact words."

"I have been obvious, Lizzy. If Jane had been half as obvious with Bingley, he would've proposed on the spot. Mr. Musgrove wouldn't think of me now even if told him I love—" She took a breath. "A thousand times, no."

"I respect Mr. Musgrove," Lizzy said, "but I don't think him subtle. It is possible he needs clarity."

"It is not done, Lizzy. Have you gone mad? A woman does not pursue a man. You refused to even hint that Jane should be more encouraging of Bingley, and now you want me to propose?"

Lizzy grimaced. "That is fair. You're right. You cannot." She smoothed her friend's chestnut brown hair where it had gotten snagged. "But perhaps I can help."

Charlotte gripped Lizzy's shoulder. "Absolutely not. It flies in the face of proper behavior, of maidenly modesty... of everything. You *cannot* speak to him."

"I won't," Lizzy says. "I am not so far lost as to put Mr. Musgrove to the blush like that. But a man could address it with him." She did not mention that Charlotte's own brother John had had a touch at him already.

"No. What man would you employ in such a thing? My father could not even address it with him unless Mr. Musgrove expressed interest. And Lizzy, I am engaged."

"True, that is the hardest part. But a friend could broach it with him. Gentlemen, I am learning, can have quite a profound impact upon one another's romances."

Charlotte frowned. "*Lizzy.*"

"Don't be afraid," said Lizzy. "I won't do anything you'd dislike."

And she wouldn't. Lizzy would not risk either of their reputations among their friends and community. She would employ...someone a bit removed, but who would, she hoped, do her a favor.

# { 18 }

I F LIZZY THOUGHT FOR A MOMENT of enlisting Mr. Darcy in her last, desperate effort to help Charlotte, she discarded it at once.

She blushed as she lay in bed Sunday morning contemplating the scenario. Ask a favor of Mr. Darcy? Share intimate details of Charlotte's feelings and Lizzy's involvement? A terrible idea.

No, no, she had another gentleman in mind. A man already thinking about love, already nearly connected with their family, and already friends with Charles Musgrove.

Bingley.

Of course, Lizzy had yet to see him again since his return from London. That made things a little awkward, but she would probably see Mr. Bingley and Mr. Darcy in church today, and almost definitely this evening if her mother invited them to supper.

Jane was happily restored to health, and though she had not gone to the Longs' party, she was readying herself for church as usual. She tied her warm, wool-lined hat on beneath her chin with a red ribbon. Her cheeks were rather flushed.

Lizzy laid a hand on her forehead. "You are not feverish again, are you?"

"I don't think so." Jane's mouth wavered.

"Is it Mr. Bingley?"

"No. That is, he may not be at the service today."

"I think he will. Have hope. I am certain he still cares about you." Lizzy had not told Jane of her conversation with Mr. Darcy; she wanted Jane and Bingley to reconcile first. But she also didn't want her sister sick with nerves or self-doubt.

"I don't want him to be there. It is wicked to wish him out of church, but people will *stare* so! It puts so much pressure on him. How unpleasant and unfair for him!"

"I think he can handle the stress for a few Sundays. Once he makes his intentions known—which I truly believe will not take more than a month or two!—there will be nothing to stare at."

"It is terrible that he cannot come back to his own house, legally leased to him, without all this speculation."

"I doubt he has heard any speculation. We hear it because of our mother and others, but he will not. Take heart, Jane."

Despite her worry, Jane looked beautiful. Her deep blue spencer jacket contrasted with her white dress, pale straw hat, and the rich red ribbon that was woven through the straw and tied in a bow just to the left of her chin.

Lizzy kissed her cheek. "Take heart, Jane," she repeated.

AT THE VILLAGE CHURCH, the Netherfield pew was no longer empty, but instead held Mr. Darcy and Mr. Bingley. It was four rows up and on the other side of the small sanctuary, but Mr. Bingley glanced over his shoulder more than once.

Growing spots of pink bloomed in his cheeks.

Jane knotted and unknotted her gloved fingers, until Lizzy firmly took one hand in hers.

Mr. Darcy, she noted, did not turn his head once. A few times his eyes followed Bingley, and he *almost* looked back, only to catch himself and face forward.

The Lucases took up a pew and a half just ahead of them, and Charlotte looked more plain, pale, and serious than usual. Poor Charlotte! She would marry Mr. Collins before the end of the year if Mr. Musgrove did not come through.

Mr. Musgrove sat with the Longs—also a family that took up the majority of two pews—and whether he was suffering the pangs of love, Lizzy did not know. She wished it—but he seemed more occupied in keeping the youngest Longs out of trouble. Without looking at his hands, he folded an interesting shape out of a scrap of paper from his pocket and passed it to one of them. It was passed around and accidentally undone, but he merely refolded a different shape and passed it secretly around again with a tell-tale quiver of laughter in the corner of his mouth.

Was it possible for such a sweet, prosaic man to be swept away by love? For he would have to be, in order to offer for Charlotte. The only other motive to offer for a lady older than himself and far less eligible would be pity, and Lizzy thought Charlotte might be better off with Mr. Collins than as the pitied wife of a man she loved.

Lizzy started when Jane reached for her hands. Lizzy had begun her own finger twisting. She and Jane were an anxious pair today and no mistake.

After the service, Lizzy's mother wasted no time in approaching Mr. Bingley. "We are so happy to see you back, sir! Are we not, Jane? We are. You must come to dinner with us—you and dear Mr. Darcy—if he will." She nodded genially to Mr. Darcy, who blinked in surprise at this unexpectedly warm greeting. He looked faintly appalled.

Mrs. Bennet was infinitely willing to be pleased with two such quarry within her sight. "We would be delighted to have you, and I know you enjoy our cook, so you can't stand on ceremony with us. You must come!" Instead of a pleasantry, this came out more as a threat.

Lizzy winced.

Mrs. Bennet realized Jane had not followed her down the aisle but remained in their pew and she gestured with her round arm. "Come, my dear, don't stand there in that stupid way! We are happy to see Mr. Bingley returned to the neighborhood, are we not?"

Jane cast a desperate glance at Lizzy as she obeyed the summons. Lizzy stayed beside her.

"We are glad to see you both," Lizzy said, with a polite dip of her head.

"Yes, very," Jane said. "I hope the... foul weather won't hinder your Christmas plans."

"Not at all!" said Bingley. "We're not bothered by a little rain, are we, Darcy? I heard you were quiet sick, Miss Bennet, but you look well again."

"Oh, yes." Jane smiled, but she was too uncomfortable to make much conversation.

Lizzy could reluctantly admit that Mr. Darcy's previous mistake was not ridiculous. With their mother's overeager manner contrasted against Jane's reserved one, it did look as if Jane might only be responding to pressure.

"What are your plans for Christmas?" Mrs. Bennet asked. She had blocked the entrance to the gentlemen's pew, quite trapping them between the wood benches and the wall.

Bingley didn't seem to mind, but Darcy was shifting his weight.

"Mama," Lizzy said, "you haven't let them answer about supper yet."

"Oh, yes, to be sure! You will come today, won't you? Don't say no."

"We'd be delighted, wouldn't we, Darcy? For supper, you say?"

"Well, it may as well be dinner, as a matter of fact!" Mrs. Bennet said. "I've had my cook roast a goose and if we don't eat it now, we'll eat it for supper. It's yours either way!"

Bingley laughed, a little silly. "Well, better sooner than later, I always say."

Lizzy's whole body wanted to crumple at her mother's needless and tasteless toadying. At least Bingley was only looking at Jane's smile. Lizzy linked arms with her mother, edging her away. "Excellent, Mr. Bingley, thank you. We'll go now to make sure all is ready."

"Oh, to be sure," Mrs. Bennet agreed. "Just come straight over. You must treat our home as your own! Lizzy, how you do tug at me. It is quite unnecessary and strange."

Lizzy felt her own cheeks flushing as they left.

Bingley and Darcy walked back to Netherfield to fetch their horses. The church was only a mile from Netherfield, but Longbourn was three. It made more sense to get their horses and ride over.

The clouds were still thick, but it was no longer raining, just a hang-dog mist that slowly sank into their coats.

"The Bennets would offer their carriage for our return," Bingley said, "I'm sure they would. But I don't mind a walk after sitting for church."

"Yes."

"You needn't go today. I won't hold it against you. I decided to come back on my own, and you don't have to hold my hand if you don't wish to have dinner with the Bennets. I'll make your excuses."

Darcy was tempted. Being addressed as *dear Mr. Darcy* by Mrs. Bennet had made his blood run cold. Had she heard that he accompanied Lizzy to the apothecary? Probably she had, the town was rife with gossip. He acquitted Lizzy of guilt, for he had seen her efforts to smooth things over in church, but it was a bit of a stumbling block.

Yes, he liked Elizabeth Bennet. Rather excessively, in fact, and it had not at all dissipated during his time in London. If anything, compared to Miss Elliot or even Miss Bingley, he was even more persuaded in her favor.

Her family was... difficult, but he did not want to be the ungentlemanly, arrogant man that Bingley had pointed out to him. Darcy had faced his faults and was trying.

But *dear* Mr. Darcy!

"If your shudder is anything to go by, I think they'd prefer you didn't come," Bingley said. "They're not that bad. You're too fastidious."

"I merely had a chill."

Bingley looked at him skeptically, wiping mist from his face and shaking off his hat before putting it back on.

"I didn't have a chill," Darcy admitted. "But yes, I will go. Perhaps you're right."

"That's the spirit. Mrs. Bennet is a bit much, but you intimidate her."

"Good." Then Darcy shook his head. "Old habits die hard. I will try not to intimidate her, I suppose. Perhaps I will try to talk to Mr. Bennet."

"*He* intimidates *me*," Bingley said. "He always has a hidden chuckle in his eyes, and I feel I must've done something quite foolish to cause it. And if he speaks of books, I do not know the authors, and if he speaks of philosophy, I do not know the thinkers."

"He's never talked to me about either."

"Perhaps because you have never felt so foolish you tried to start a conversation about a book he'd set aside!"

"Well, that is very foolish, if you don't know the book."

Bingley punched him in the arm.

"What violence," Darcy said. "Miss Bennet would be shocked."

Bingley found, after a meal of roasted goose, wild rice, boiled potatoes, honeyed carrots, and a sticky Christmas fruit cake, that he was both full and happy.

It was not yet Christmas, but perhaps Mrs. Bennet thought it was close enough for fruitcake. He was full because of the meal. He was happy because of Jane.

She really was the most beautiful woman he'd ever met, and she was sweet and kind. With her, he felt like he was ready to settle down at Netherfield and learn to be a responsible landowner. She made him brave.

Brave enough to sit beside her when the family retired from the table to the rear parlor, and brave enough not to worry when he realized he'd been talking almost exclusively with her for half an hour.

The others had left them alone, and even Darcy didn't look upset. Miss Elizabeth had challenged him to a game of chess at the corner table near the window. It kept his mind busy and prevented anyone from chattering at him. Bingley silently thanked her for it.

Lydia and Kitty, pouting but resigned, had settled down with samplers under their mother's unusually stern eye. Mary had excused herself to practice the pianoforte in the front parlor.

The only question that remained was how soon he could ask Jane to marry him. Probably today was too soon. Perhaps tomorrow.

"I do believe the sun has finally come out," Mrs. Bennet said. "You young people ought to go for a walk, or at least a turn in the shrubbery."

Kitty and Lydia threw their work down at once, and Jane smiled at Bingley. "Would you care to? If you and Mr. Darcy have business to attend to, however, we understand. You have already given us a large part of the afternoon."

"I have nothing that needs doing on a Sunday," Bingley declared.

Darcy and Lizzy were still seated next to the chess board. Darcy appeared not to hear the proposal. He studied the board and finally gave a half-smile. "There it is."

"Never."

He moved his bishop, palming Miss Elizabeth's knight, and placing his bishop two places diagonal from her queen. "Checkmate."

"Ugh. Is it checkmate? My rook—no, I see you are right. How detestable in you to win as soon as there is prospect of going outside. Have you merely been waiting to finish me off?" She rose from the table and shook her crumpled skirt out.

"No, I never throw a game." Darcy looked about him and seemed surprised that everyone was standing. "Are we going out? I wouldn't mind a stretch."

Soon they were all in the Bennets' garden, which had the advantage of overgrown hedges and tall screens of sturdy, dark-green winter foliage. Enough to give privacy, should one care to have it.

Bingley was thinking perhaps today *was* a good day for a proposal—the sunlight was making the raindrops sparkle, and women liked that sort of thing, didn't they? He might as well ask her, mightn't he?

Lizzy whispered to Jane, "I need to talk to Mr. Bingley. Would you object to falling behind with Mr. Darcy for just a few minutes?"

Jane avoided a puddle. "Oh, but—"

"Please, Jane."

"I suppose so. Lizzy, you aren't up to mischief?"

"No more than usual, and nothing to make you blush."

Having shaken off Lydia, who stuck out her tongue, but tramped away with Kitty, Lizzy turned to Bingley.

"It is too narrow here. Will you walk a stretch with me, Mr. Bingley? I haven't heard news of your sister— I do hope she is having a pleasant time in Bath."

"Er—yes, I believe so. I had a letter from her yesterday—"

"Excellent, you can tell me how she is."

He looked a little scattered at this query, his thoughts were clearly elsewhere, but he was too kind and well-behaved to make it awkward. He held out his arm and grinned. "I'm afraid Bath has terrible weather in December—I told her it would be so—but they have found much to do."

Jane took Mr. Darcy's offered arm and hoped Lizzy appreciated it. Mr. Darcy was rather stern, and Jane would have much preferred to walk with Mr. Bingley. Lizzy knew that, of course, which made this all the more strange.

Jane had been fearful that seeing Mr. Bingley after these weeks would be embarrassing, but it had quickly faded. By the time Bingley sat beside her in the parlor, it had almost been as if he'd never left.

Mr. Darcy, however—she had never quite gotten his measure.

Darcy steered Jane around a pile of wet leaves. "I had not thought Caroline and your sister were particularly close. But I'm not much of a judge."

Jane blushed. They certainly were not close. Lizzy had said very unkind things about Caroline and her pride. Jane believed that Caroline's harsh letter to herself was out of love for her brother, but Lizzy had had no patience with that.

"I—Perhaps they—Not particularly," Jane admitted.

"Ah." Mr. Darcy kicked a winter bramble out of the path. "An honest answer."

"Of course."

"You'd be surprised. Not all young ladies, or young men for that matter, are honest."

"I think people generally intend to be honest, but sometimes they are too scared or too hurt to do so."

"Do you not believe in wrongdoing, Miss Bennet?"

"Yes, but—I think there is very much less of it than people are prone to suspect. Lizzy says I am hopelessly optimistic, but I think we must make allowances for deficits of understanding or action that aren't malicious."

"You've given this some thought."

"I don't think one could be friends with Lizzy and *not* give thought."

"Given then that you are thoughtful and honest, what scheme is your sister hatching with my friend?"

Jane laughed uncertainly—was Mr. Darcy actually joking with her? This was the friendliest conversation she'd shared with him by far. "I am in the dark, sir, I promise."

Lizzy listened as Bingley told her a few details about Caroline's trip: rain, rooms near the Royal Pavilion, concerts.

"It sounds wet but otherwise enjoyable," Lizzy said. "I hope she'll have an excellent time with Sir Walter and Miss Elliot."

"Thank you!" He looked behind him in a shifty fashion and increased their pace slightly. "Since we have a moment, I would like to clear something up."

Lizzy was nonplussed. *She* was the one with an agenda this afternoon, not Bingley.

"The thing is," he said, "I saw the letter you sent Caroline. Very kind of you to be concerned for her, but the rumors about Darcy are all rot. Wickham is a liar and worse—but how would you know that? You don't seem to be cutting up stiff with Darcy, which I appreciate, but I don't want you to labor under a false view of him. He's cleared up some things with the tradesmen in Meryton, but he won't clear himself for his own benefit, it's not his way."

"Oh. You don't need to tell me—"

"But I do. You were also wrong about him and Caroline—well, you've been sadly misinformed on a number of issues! Thing is, I haven't seen him smile as much as I have lately and I think—well, mum for that. How I do rattle on! In short, I like things in the open and Darcy can be a mule at times, but he's rock solid."

Lizzy made what she could of this somewhat inarticulate explanation. "Thank you for explaining. I had already begun to suspect that Wickham was playing a false game, and now I am confirmed. You are a good friend to Mr. Darcy." She was also, quite against her will, interested to hear that Mr. Bingley did not think Mr. Darcy was going to marry his sister.

But that was not the point, and she really must focus.

"I try to be a good friend." Bingley slowed his steps. "Shall we rejoin them?"

"Actually, since we are exchanging confidences, I had a question about your friend—about Mr. Musgrove."

"Oh, Muskie—yes, he's going home tomorrow, isn't he? He called on me yesterday. I wish his stay had overlapped longer with mine! Best of good chaps."

"Yes. He is a very agreeable man and—although it is none of my business exactly—I was wondering whether he said anything to you about... Well, if perhaps he mentioned..." Lizzy found her sense of propriety put up a stronger fight than she expected.

"Oh dear, this is uncomfortable." Lizzy shook her head. "You are the soul of patience, Mr. Bingley. Do you think Mr. Musgrove might've formed an attachment during his stay?"

Bingley opened his mouth. Closed it. Furrowed his handsome brow. "I am not aware of it if he did. We only talked commonplaces. The hunting, the Longs and Lucases, our school days." He glanced back at Darcy and Jane. "Er, I take it you might—that is, Muskie is the best of good blokes—were you hoping..." He stuttered to a stop, turning a bit red.

"Oh! I am an idiot today. *No,* I like Mr. Musgrove very well, but I have no designs on the poor man. Poor Mr. Bingley, you are too good! I was wondering, in fact, if he mentioned my friend Charlotte, that is, Miss Lucas?"

Bingley laughed. "That is a relief! Yes, I think he did. Let me think, we were talking about the Elliots, and then what an affable family the Lucases are... I danced with Miss Lucas first when we came to that assembly in Meryton—do you recall? I was quite bowled over by—by your sister, and Miss Lucas was kind. She's droll, too, cleverer than I. I like her."

"Yes, as do I, she's one of my closest friends. But Mr. Musgrove—"

"Oh, indeed. He asked if I'd met the parson she's going to wed at Christmas time, but I hadn't really. Saw him in passing while he was here, I suppose. Caroline said he was the most vain and obsequious little toady— oh sorry! I do rattle on. Don't mean half what I say."

Bingley was so beautifully innocent, Lizzy wondered if she would have to spell it out further.

She turned them to the right, to walk out of the shrubbery and along the line of chestnuts.

Mr. Bingley's blue eyes widened. "Oh. Oh, I see. I am not the quickest chap. Do you mean to say *Muskie* and *Miss Lucas*? Ain't she engaged?"

"Yes, but she entered it too quickly. I know it is shocking, but I cannot help thinking if ever an engagement were better to be broken, this might be it."

"It *is* a lady's prerogative."

"Practically the only thing we *can* decide," Lizzy agreed. "But do you think there's any chance Mr. Musgrove would be interested in Miss Lucas? You needn't fear to wound me—or her!—for I know this is terribly indelicate, and I will never breathe a word."

"Never mind about the apologies. I just told you I'm the sort who likes everything laid out. And if you were going to talk to anyone," he blushed slightly, "who better than someone who'll be a...a brother to you someday, Lord willing!"

"Oh!" Lizzy pressed his arm with excitement. "I should be honored to have you as a brother."

"I hadn't meant to say anything, but I can hardly wait—well, mum for that too. Let me think on your question." He sucked his lips in as he sank deep into thought.

Lizzy steered Mr. Bingley toward the lake path. She glanced back at Darcy and Jane. They still seemed to be talking as they walked under the intermittent shadow of the bare chestnut trees. Poor Jane! Lizzy had quite cut her out on this walk, but Jane would have Bingley for the rest of her life. Charlotte only had two weeks.

"I think they would suit capitally," Mr. Bingley said, "and I think—now that I am alert to it—that he is concerned for Miss Lucas. That's a good sign, yes?"

"Yes. A very good sign. Unfortunately, it is impossible for her to speak to him, and I do not know Mr. Musgrove well. You, as a friend, might speak to him..."

He grinned. "Oh, so it is not just information, but also a favor you want? You are already acting like a sister."

"I will owe you deeply."

He waved a hand. "Nonsense. I am so happy—stupidly happy, Darcy would probably say—that I can't help but want it for my friends. Muskie is an excellent chap. He'll probably end up with the youngest Elliot girl if nothing is done; he said as much the other day. That's not what I'd wish for him."

"Thank you, Mr. Bingley. Whether anything comes of it is not in our hands, but I appreciate talking to a sensible man about such matters."

"Darcy," Bingley called, "did you hear that? She called me a sensible man."

"She has clearly gotten fatigued and delusional."

Bingley puffed up dramatically. "An insult to Miss Elizabeth and myself? I'm affronted. A meeting at dawn."

"You are more likely to oversleep than I."

Bingley deflated, laughing. "I am. Shall we turn back, Miss Bennet?"

Jane took Bingley's offered arm. "Mr. Darcy and I were just discussing how far you planned to go."

"I apologize," Lizzy said, "that was my doing, but you know how I love a good walk."

Mr. Darcy raised a quizzical eyebrow. "Was it a good walk?"

"Enlightening and helpful; Mr. Bingley is the definition of chivalry." Lizzy rested her gloved hand on Darcy's forearm. "Shall we?"

# { 19 }

IF ANY OTHER LADY HAD MONOPOLIZED Bingley on a semi-private walk as Lizzy had just done, Darcy would've protected him.

Thankfully, Darcy did not doubt Lizzy's love for her sister or suspect that she harbored amorous feelings for Bingley.

He *was* rather curious what she wanted to say to him, however.

Her cheeks were pink with suppressed excitement, and it was only with difficulty that she slowed her pace with his to let Jane and Bingley move ahead with a modicum of privacy. The strong trunks of the chestnut trees rose up to his left. Lizzy didn't avoid the brown patches of moldering leaves as they walked, but kicked through them with satisfaction.

Was she truly going to give no explanation?

"I have not been this curious about a secret since I was at Harrow," Darcy admitted.

"I *am* sorry. I'm afraid I cannot satisfy your curiosity, for I have already indulged in an egregious piece of meddling. It would be too bad of me to continue. It would definitely verge on gossip."

"But it does not count as gossip with Bingley? I hesitate to inform you that he is not *precisely* the soul of discretion."

"Are you jealous of your friend?" Lizzy laughed. "Perhaps it will make you feel better to know that, in general, I believe you would be better at keeping a confidence than Mr. Bingley. You have only to be yourself, and you will say nothing! In this specific instance, however, you would not be able to do anything about the matter, and Mr. Bingley may."

"My pride was not wounded, I was merely, as I said, curious."

Lizzy spied that Jane and Bingley had taken a turn into the shrubbery ahead. The turn was away from the house. "Will you be perturbed if Mr. Bingley proposes to Jane today? I rather think he might."

"Not at all. I fully expect it by the time we leave Longbourn."

"He does like to do things in a rush. I thought he was being silly when he said that he does everything all at once, but perhaps there was more truth there than I thought."

"He doesn't tend to deliberate overly long, but in this instance he *has* given it much thought."

"If they marry, I suppose I will see you at Netherfield now and again. Perhaps you may grow to like Hertfordshire after all, Mr. Darcy."

"I don't *dis*like it."

Elizabeth was so beautiful today, it was distracting. He could not help thinking that with Jane and Bingley in the shrubbery, he was now alone with her.

"Are you sure? You certainly have not evinced much enjoyment of Hertfordshire."

"I see no need to make a display of emotion," Darcy said. "If I like a thing, it is enough for *me* to know it; I feel no need to tell everyone."

"Yes, it's terribly vulgar to display happiness or joy. It might make people think they know you. I never do so if I can help it."

"I was just complimenting your sister on her honesty, but I don't think I can say the same for you." He smiled. "You enjoy saying the opposite of what you think."

"Me? Never."

Mr. Bingley tucked Jane's arm a little closer with his own, bringing himself a half-step nearer. They turned to the right into a lane of the shrubbery that ran perpendicular to the first. Another turn brought them to a parallel row, where they were temporarily out of sight of house and friends. The bushes dripped and murmured like a conversation a long way off.

"Your sister is very loyal to her friends," Bingley said.

"Yes, Lizzy is kind-hearted, but I don't know what she wanted to speak to you about. If it was about me, I hope you will forget it. There is no pressure—no expectation—"

"I hesitate to interrupt you, but you must not worry. She said nothing about you. She did make me very happy though." He took Jane's hand in his own rather than letting it rest on his arm as was proper. It was only natural to interlock their fingers and bring her to a stop.

"Jane, I—I told your sister that I would very much like to be her brother. Her answer gave me hope that I have not mucked it all up too far. Would you marry me? I love everything about you, but I'm not very good at pretty speeches. You are the most kind and beautiful girl I have ever met. I want to be with you forever. I wanted to ask you before, but then I disappeared for weeks without a word. If you are angry with me, I understand. And I was going to wait for a few more weeks, but the—you like raindrops, don't you?"

A growing smile lit her face. "Raindrops?"

"I mean—raindrops, sunshine—this is the kind of pretty day on which a woman likes to be proposed to, isn't it? *Will* you marry me?"

Jane's eyes were shining with tears. "Yes, I would be honored to marry you."

Bingley beamed, but then Darcy's words came to mind, and he grew uncertain. Were those happy tears or not? *Did* her mother influence her?

"The honor would be mine, but I don't want you to feel that you must accept. I know your mother would like it, but I won't say a word if you'd rather I didn't. I want you to be *happy*, not—not—honored."

Jane shook her head, smiling even wider. "You are the most considerate of men. I am happy. I am *so* happy. My mother's opinion matters not at all, except that I am glad my parents will rejoice with me."

"Phew. That's all well, then." He held both her hands. "I don't suppose... Before Darcy catches up..."

Jane tilted her head up to see him better, and Bingley leaned down to press his lips to hers.

NOT MORE THAN HALF a mile away, Wickham kissed Mary Elliot in a vastly different frame of mind.

He was grateful in his own way, but he was far from incandescent happiness.

The carriage he'd hired to get them to London was tawdry and cheap—by necessity—and it rather smelled of mold. The lodgings he would get in town would also be lackluster, though he would avoid the river district if he could—he doubted Mary would appreciate the smell of the Thames.

He would have to leave his regimentals in his rooms here, and that was annoying as well. People trusted a man in colors. He'd already packed up everything else, his own knickknacks, shaving gear, and civilian clothes.

At least he wasn't leaving Meryton and the regiment empty-handed. Mary was a prime plum. Not quite as good as Miss King would've been, but a far-sight better than nothing, and a decent chance of payoff before the end.

If Mary flew the coop before he got the marriage register signed or hammered out a deal with her father, he would be in a bind. It was a calculated risk, however. He was good with women, and he would keep her on the line until the deal was settled. With a man of Sir Walter's status and wealth, Wickham wouldn't settle for less than £10,000.

Wickham broke off the kiss with an excuse. "I think I hear a wagon."

"I don't hear anything."

"Perhaps it is only my over-tired nerves." Ugh, to think he should live to sound like Mrs. Bennet. "Are you certain you are willing to run away with me? Darcy has poisoned my superior officers, my friends, everyone. I would not blame you for doubting me."

"Not me. I believe you, Wickham."

"You are a treasure. We won't be living in the comfort you are accustomed to, at least, not at first, but you would turn my despair to joy."

"What do I care for comfort?" She placed a hand on her heart.

He tried to hide his weariness with playacting. Her next sentence, however, was a twist worthy of a Drury Lane dramatist.

"All the same," she said, "I have been thinking, and I have decided you should join my family in Bath."

Wickham mentally slammed against this sudden, unexpected wall. "What?"

"Yes, just think! In Bath you may live cheaply for a little while, more cheaply than London, and you may ask my father for my hand in the regular way. Then we will be married there—how jealous my sisters will be!—and all will be right."

"That is so—generous of you. Has it occurred to you, however, that your excellent father may not support our plan?"

"Well, of course he would. I love you."

"And I you, beloved. But, er, from a pragmatic standpoint, I don't appear in the best light."

"I can bring him around. Besides, you are very handsome and that will weigh with him! He cannot stand ugly men and women. I think he will be surprised I have caught such a good-looking gentleman, and that will just *show* them."

"That's... reassuring. But have you considered the time it would take? Your father might wish to make sure you know your mind. He might ask us to wait a year—two years! I would never ask you to wait so long for poor me, nor would I expect it."

She finally looked thoughtful. "I doubt he would do anything so stupid. Still, even a year would be too long."

"Exactly. Even a month would be too long."

"If only we could run away to London, but still get married with my family! If we married alone in London with a special license, it would be so *dull*."

"A sad truth. In fact, you have hit upon an idea. We could go to London, and...and not immediately get married. We could save the festivities to have with your family in the new year."

Mary furrowed her brow. "How would that work? Father would be annoyed with me."

"Not annoyed, so much as concerned, I'm sure. His concern would translate to a rapid wedding. At Bath, if you wish." Now he really did hear a wagon, and he pulled her a few steps further into the shadow of the dripping pines.

"Do you mean—you would ruin my reputation so that Father would *have* to agree?"

"That's an unpleasant way to describe a dire necessity. I would never—"

She slapped him—though it was light, and he immediately realized she was being playful.

"Silly Wickham! That is a terrible idea. I have one much better."

He was seriously annoyed, but he locked his jaw and smiled. "Yes?"

"We go to Bath and speak to my father. If he does any of those unpleasant things you said, we simply tell him I am already ruined. It saves time and discomfort."

"I thought you didn't care about comfort."

"Wickham."

"I'm sorry, my dearest, you've taken me off-guard." Wickham tried to think. Her plan had merit—sort of— but her father might very well send him packing. For one thing, Mary was not a good liar. For another, it was different to *suspect* your daughter had been indiscreet than to have her live with a man for a few weeks. The latter was far more compelling.

Maybe Mary Elliot was not worth the effort. He would be alone in London, and one could always find company when one needed. And then he might try for another girl, an heiress in her own right... The idea already cheered him.

As if she could hear what he was thinking, Mary squared her shoulders. "I might tell him so anyway."

Wickham rocked back on his heels. "Excuse me."

"You are losing your nerve. Not that I blame you." She patted his cheek. "It is a conundrum and full of difficulties. But you don't know my father as I do, and you must learn to trust me. I will make everything right."

"Mary. If you tell your father that I—compromised you and left, he will be angry. It could ruin me. Both of us."

"He will be very angry for a moment, perhaps, but if you are there to make all right, he will come around! If you *aren't* there, I suppose he might be *more* angry, thinking you are trying to throw off your responsibility."

Wickham could not tell if she meant to threaten him or was doing it wholly by ignorance. He would be almost impressed, if he was not so horrified.

"I don't *have* any responsibility," he said. "We haven't, er, done anything."

"But he won't know that! It is perfect, Wickham. But why do you not look happy? It is perfect, unless you *don't* want to marry me? In which case, I think you *have* taken advantage of me, making me think so. I should probably tell the Lucases how ill you used me, or even Mr. Darcy, if that is the case."

Wickham stared at her. "That's—that's not what taking advantage means!"

Mary's eyes were implacable. "If you truly wish to marry me, all is simple."

Wickham admitted defeat, at least temporarily. "Of course I want to marry you. I am only in shock. I love you so madly, Mary, I can hardly think. Please forgive me."

She squealed and threw her arms around him. "Thank you, Wickham. Everything will go perfectly, don't worry."

# { 20 }

ARCY WAS LURED TO LONGBOURN again Monday evening, after having spent most of Sunday there.

Jane and Bingley's engagement meant a lavish dinner (despite the roasted goose consumed the previous day), and the house smelled of roasting ham and black truffles when they arrived.

"Capital food, you must admit," Bingley said.

"Hm."

Mrs. Bennet had invited all the families she could get on such short notice to celebrate with her. The evening was given to jollification and young people. The Lucases, Elliots, and Longs were included, with Mr. Musgrove, too, of course.

Darcy knew he could've cried off if he wanted to. Bingley would understand, and Mrs. Bennet would hardly notice—she was so wrapped up in the happy couple.

He hadn't done so. He was like a fish which swam into a trap of sharpened spikes and couldn't swim backwards. He'd come back to Hertfordshire of his own volition, swimming right into the trap he'd known awaited him.

Today he had been the recipient of Lizzy's actual smiles and goodwill—not the playful resentment he now recognized he'd received prior—and he was not strong enough to give it up.

He was little better than a trout.

Charlotte pulled Lizzy aside as soon as she arrived. The Longbourn stairs had no handy nook or alcove, but Charlotte knew Mr. Bennet's library would be empty just now.

She closed the door behind them for privacy. The fire was low, but it still gave a little warmth and light that reflected off the many books on the shelved walls.

"I cannot believe I said as much as I did at the Longs' party," Charlotte said. "I must have been more affected than I thought. You have not done anything rash, have you, Lizzy?"

"...no. Not at all."

"Oh, Lizzy! What did you do? I am going to be mortified. I am *already* mortified."

"No, you won't be, for I shan't tell you. Honestly, it was not much, and it may mean nothing. It probably *will* mean nothing, as much as I'd like otherwise."

Charlotte eyed her friend. "I hope you're right. I must have been crazy. Just promise you won't breathe another word. The only way I can live comfortably is to forget this ever happened, or that you ever knew."

"I understand."

Charlotte decided to be content with that. Pushing Lizzy never got one anywhere, and if Charlotte thought about it much more, she might be sick.


Mr. Musgrove tapped Anne's elbow in hello when the gentlemen joined the ladies after dinner. She was sat to the side of the pianoforte, where one of the Bennet girls was waiting eagerly to be asked to play.

"Are you feeling low, Anne? You look a bit pale."

"No, I'm fine. The hubbub of the engagement is just a little overpowering."

"They look happy, don't they? Bingley hasn't stopped grinning all night."

"I'm glad for them. It's a match desired on all sides; they have no detractors."

"True. Though I don't think they'd much care if they did."

"Miss Bennet would," Anne said sadly. "She might easily be persuaded to give him up and what a tragedy that would be." She shook her head. "Or maybe I wrong her, and she would hold fast to him no matter what."

The bleakness in Anne's voice was unmistakable. Musgrove suddenly wondered if he'd ever known her as well as he thought. Was there someone *else*? Is that why she turned him down?

Ah, well, it was not his business. He wouldn't make a bother of himself by asking for Anne's hand again, and that thought did not sadden him as it had last month. His attention had been taken up with Charlotte—but that was ridiculous.

Mary Elliot came up to them, looking like a cat who'd found cream. "Good evening, Mr. Musgrove. A very fine night, is it not?"

"Yes, looks to be clear and starry."

"I hope we have a good, fast trip to Bath. You must say hello to your mother and sisters for me when you return home. I daresay they will not ask about us, but you must tell them that they shall hear exceptionally good news of *me* soon."

"Shall they?" Anne said. "I should like some good news, please share."

"No, no. It's a surprise for Bath. Oh, I *cannot* wait."

Mr. Musgrove smiled. "That's more like it. Nice to see you looking cheerful."

"I'm sure I'm always cheerful when I have reason. I am not stupidly cheerful like some girls, but you will never see me pining away and moping."

Anne and he maintained a discreet silence that she could take as agreement if she wished.

"No," Mary continued, "I am learning to make things happen the way I want. All it takes is a little resolution. Have you not told me so, Anne?"

"Yes, I have, but resolution is only as good as its aim." She looked expressively at Mr. Musgrove. "Please excuse us for a moment."

Musgrove assumed she wanted to get to the bottom of Mary's excitement, and she probably ought to do so. Mary was a good girl, but not as steady as Anne.

Once again the library was put to use, though Anne did not feel very secure in using it and didn't latch the door. The fire was down to embers, but the winter moon was enough to illuminate Mary's features.

"I must ask what your elliptical statements mean," Anne said. "I am concerned for you."

"Nothing you need to worry your head about. I fancy I have found an excellent solution."

"You're scaring me, Mary. You wouldn't—wouldn't run away with Lieutenant Wickham, would you?"

"Anne! How could you even ask that?"

"I'm sorry. I love you, Mary, and I don't want to see you deceived."

"Deceived? You said you would support Wickham's suit!"

"If you have a true preference for him, yes, but I fear he is not as steady as we hoped."

"I think you've confused the definition of *steady* with *dead.*"

"Only promise me that you will not do anything rash. Don't sneak out of the Lucases house or—or anything of that sort."

"How *dare* you accuse me of clandestine behavior! You never understood me. I can't wait to be back with Father and Elizabeth." Mary flounced out.

Anne pressed cold fingers to her trembling lips. Perhaps if her mother had lived, Lady Elliot would have known how to handle Mary. Anne certainly did not.

Bingley was having one of the happiest nights of his life. Was there ever such an exquisite angel as Jane Bennet? Was there ever such a warm, welcoming family as the Bennets?

He'd said as much to Darcy as the tea tray was brought in.

"Go soak your head," Darcy recommended.

Bingley only laughed. Despite his perfect enjoyment, he did notice Lizzy giving him a glance every now and then.

Ah, yes. He had promised to speak to Muskie. He'd thought it might be a trifle odd or awkward, but at the moment, nothing seemed easier! What could be more natural?

"I say, want to step to the library and have a cigar?" Bingley asked him.

"What? Do you smoke cigars now?" Muskie asked.

"Oh. No, I don't, forgot about that. Do you?"

"On occasion."

"Capital, this can be one of those occasions. Do come." Bingley had seen Mr. Bennet lean back in a corner of the parlor with a book, so he knew the library was empty.

Bingley's chat with Mr. Bennet had gone quite well, and Bingley hadn't even been put to the blush. Mr. Bennet had at once guessed the purpose of his library visit on Sunday, and he had assured him all was well. Jane would have her thousand pounds from her mother, and Bingley had settled nine more on her, bringing it to ten. Bingley had been prepared if Mr. Bennet wanted it to be more, but Darcy had been right that it fit the size of his fortune. That would give Jane three or four hundred pounds a year in interest, which she could use for herself, her family expenses, or reinvestment.

The fire in the library had died down to coals now, and Bingley used the iron tongs to put another log on. He fanned it for a moment, and he was pleased to see a yellow orange flicker as it caught and crackled.

"Do you have a cigar?" Muskie asked.

"Eh? Oh, no, I didn't think of that either."

His friend laughed. "Then perhaps you'd better just tell me what you wanted to say, and you can go back to admiring Miss Bennet."

"Ha, you're a good chap. Always were."

"Thank you. Likewise." Muskie looked at the walls of books with faint wonder. "Lot of books here, eh? I should feel guilty all the time if this was mine."

"I know. Quite dizzies my head, but Darcy says he's got a good collection." Bingley twisted his lips in thought. "I don't think Jane is a great reader."

"Does that bother you?"

"What? No! I meant it in a good way. She says her next sister, Miss Lizzy, is more studious, which wouldn't do for me. I quite wonder if she's caught Darcy's eye, though."

Muskie raised his brows. "Did you really bring me into the library to gossip about your friend Darcy?"

"No, about you! That is, to gossip about you. You know what I mean."

"I truly don't."

"It's Miss Lizzy—she's the one who asked me to speak to you."

Muskie squinted at him. "Are you on the toddle? Had a bit more than a splash?"

"What? No!"

"The Bennets seem like a comfortable family unit, but I have no intention of marrying into it, even if it would make us brothers-in-law. You must be content with your own match."

"No, no—I thought this would be easy but I'm doing it so badly. Thing is: Charlotte Lucas. You should marry her; it'd make you happy. She's a capital young lady."

Muskie sat abruptly on the chair beside him. "What?"

"Miss Lucas, you know. If you like her, you should offer for her."

"I—I can't *offer* for her; she's engaged to that parson."

"I know, the one Caroline says is a slimy, self-important toad. Miss Lucas could cry off from it."

"I suppose she could—but would she want to? Are you sure?"

Bingley pictured Lizzy's face. "Sure as sure."

Musgrove was silent, unusual worry lines marking his square, cheerful face.

"Well," Bingley said. "What do you think?"

"I don't know. I enjoy talking to Miss Lucas, as who wouldn't? She is comforting and practical, and really quite pretty. She has a way of looking that makes me feel... brave. Do I sound like an idiot, Bingley?"

"As a matter of fact, no. I know what you mean."

"But it would cause *such* a noise. Sounds like a melodrama my sisters would like, not something *I'd* do. Especially if she doesn't particularly care... Are you sure Miss Lucas would say yes? You can't be. Surely she didn't speak to you."

"No, nothing like that. I don't think she knows anything about it, but Miss Lizzy was convincing. Dash it all, I'm happy, and I like to see other people happy. You think it through, but I'm off to the party. You were joking, but I *do* want to go back to admiring Jane."

Bingley went back to the parlor with the satisfaction of a job done well, if not perfectly.

He smiled at Miss Lizzy and planted himself again next to Jane.

Lizzy felt nearly ill with anxiety after watching Mr. Musgrove disappear for a few minutes with Mr. Bingley.

She noted—thank heavens—that Charlotte did not see them. Lizzy had purposely suggested a game of lottery for Lydia and Kitty and the young Lucas boys. Then she all but manhandled Charlotte to the table to be in charge of the game. Lizzy had even managed to get Charlotte into the chair that faced the dark windows and drapes, rather than facing into the parlor toward the doors.

Mr. Bingley smiled at her when he returned, but Lizzy was so anxious it did not help.

She desperately hoped she had not embarrassed her friend and angered or disgusted Mr. Musgrove. She'd been confident of her read on his character, but now she was questioning everything.

Mr. Darcy was an excellent example. She'd thought she had a clear understanding of his character, and hadn't he been a surprise?

There was Mr. Darcy now, coming back from the tea tray with a fresh cup. She had not liked him at first, thinking him proud and unpleasant. Now she still thought him proud, yes, but with a willingness to unbend and a sense of humor she had not expected.

Clearly, her ability to analyze character traits was not as strong as she'd thought.

Mr. Darcy extended the teacup to her when he reached her. "It seems you have not received a cup yet, Miss Elizabeth."

"Oh, is this for me? Thank you." Jane was pouring out, but Lizzy had been too tense to approach the small throng around her.

"Not at all." He clasped his hands behind his back. "It tastes better if you drink it warm."

Lizzy took a dutiful sip. There was Mr. Musgrove coming back to the parlor, and she coughed a little. Where would he go? Would he speak to Charlotte? Had she been as foolish as she suspected?

"Are you ever anxious, Mr. Darcy?"

"Not often. It is not a productive feeling to indulge. Any decision at all is usually better than an unmade one that preys on the mind."

Mr. Musgrove took a cup of tea from Jane and stood a little apart from the others.

"You sound as if you know."

Did Mr. Darcy look self-conscious? "There *is* one decision weighing on my mind," he said. "Although I would describe myself as uncertain, rather than anxious."

Lizzy raised her teacup. "To mental fortitude."

She took another deep swallow of tea. It was late, and soon the party would break up. She did not know what to hope for.

Mr. Musgrove moved to stand nearer to the lottery table, looking over young John Lucas's shoulder and offering a word or two of advice. It also moved him into Charlotte's view.

Charlotte, to do her credit, showed no self-consciousness. She continued to collect tickets and deal cards to the young people as they exclaimed or groaned at their small wins and losses.

Mr. Darcy realized he had lost Lizzy's attention.

She still stood next to him, her arm nearly brushing his, but her eyes were fixed on the table of rowdy young men and women, or perhaps on her friend, Miss Lucas.

It was true that he had a decision to make, and that decision was whether or not to propose to Miss Elizabeth.

It touched his sense of humor that she had stumbled so near to it, only to completely miss the hint. Miss Bingley or Miss Elliot would have followed up, he was sure. Possibly Lizzy would have as well, if she was not distracted by some care tonight.

Darcy was startled by Mrs. Bennet bumping his elbow rather roughly. He stepped to the side. "Excuse me, ma'am."

"No, no, Mr. Darcy. It's my clumsy feet! But how can I be agile when I am so happy? Not but what I used to be *very* agile; I met Mr. Bennet at a ball! I wish we could have dancing tonight, but I didn't have James move the furniture out to make space. I'm sure I don't know what I was thinking. Jane and dear Mr. Bingley would enjoy it."

"They seem fine."

"Fie, Mr. Darcy, you are so droll! Of course they are more than fine, they are engaged! So humorous."

Mr. Darcy withheld his wince at her arch, teasing tone. She moved on.

Lizzy was making the wince that he felt, but she did not say anything. What could she say? It was silly to apologize for other people, and she was not the one at fault. Bingley was right, too. Mrs. Bennet was gauche and fawning, but she was not a terror.

The lottery game broke up, and Mr. Musgrove rounded the table to Mr. Bennet. "Excuse me, sir, but could I trouble you for a piece of paper? Just any scrap."

This had to be repeated, since Mr. Bennet was lost in his book.

"What? Oh, for the game?" he said vaguely. "There is paper in the library. Lizzy can fetch it."

"Oh, I'll do so myself, if you don't mind," he said. "No need to put her out."

Darcy felt as if he was watching a play. They were all actors, and only Lizzy knew the script. She might, judging by her tenseness, have *written* the script.

When the lottery game broke up, Charlotte collected the cards and fish and put them in the small, leather pouch. She tied the strings and left them on the table.

She ventured to hope she'd made a tempest out of a teakettle. Mr. Musgrove had watched the last third of the game, but he looked in no way annoyed or strange.

All was calm, and he would leave Meryton tomorrow with the Elliots.

A fresh pot of tea had just been brought in and the room smelled of warm bodies, fire, and good black tea. Mary Bennet was finally allowed to play piano while everyone finished their tea, and Charlotte breathed in relief. The party would break up soon.

Mary's playing was ambitious, and she was playing a song with many trills, runs, and flurries of notes. Unfortunately, she did not have much in the way of dynamics, and her only goal was to be noticed. It was loud.

Charlotte did not feel more than a slight frisson of unease when Mr. Musgrove joined her on the settee. There could be no easy conversation over the sound of the pianoforte. She smiled at him and turned to face in Mary's general direction again.

Mr. Musgrove chose a moment to speak to her when Mary was fingering her way more slowly through an arpeggio run.

"Miss Lucas."

She looked at him in question, and realized he was handing her a small piece of paper down low, near his waist. The paper was cream-colored and torn on one edge, folded into a neat square.

She took it. Did his full cheeks look a bit more flushed than usual?

He rose and moved away, ostensibly to pick up one of the fish from the game which had fallen on the floor. Its sparkling mother-of-pearl finish reflected the candlelight.

Charlotte's heartbeat pulsed in her ears and down to her toes as she tucked the small paper into a fold of her skirt. She could not even speculate as to what it might say. Surely he would not have written a goodbye note?

She felt giddy and light-headed. As if any moment might tip her back into the largely dun-colored world she'd lived in until she fell for Mr. Musgrove. Right now the fire was bright, every dress seemed like it had been drawn directly from a stripe of a rainbow, and every lip and eye held sparkling color.

She waited a moment and then rose and slipped out the door to the hall. She had heard Mary play this piece before, and knew it lasted a solid forty-five minutes, bless the girl.

The library was warmer than it had been, with a fresh log partially burnt and still going merrily. In fact, the fire was too good. She glanced around with a hand at her throat to see if someone else was present.

She felt more as if she were contemplating a heinous crime instead of reading a note. Mr. Bennet's oil lamp was on his desk, and Charlotte turned the small brass knob to lengthen the wick and pumped the small button three times to force the oil upwards into the well.

With this light, she finally spread out the paper.

*Miss Lucas,*

*I have already told you that my family is not at all elegant, only happy. Therefore, please forgive this irregularity.*

*The thought that you might be heading toward a future that is short on comfort and friendship has been plaguing my mind. Though we have only been acquainted a little less than a month, I respect your sense, economy, and kindness. I also enjoy your company and have had a far more pleasant trip than I expected—mainly due to you. I don't know how it is—or if it is perhaps a selfish love of comfort—but I feel that you would add greatly to my comfort, and I hope, I would to yours also. I believe that we should be very happy with one another.*

*If this idea is repugnant to you, please simply burn this letter and no more need be said.*

*If it is not, I am at your disposal. I find I am more particular than I thought I was in the matter of my future companionship, and you are the person I want for it. Perhaps you might return this note with your answer before the end of the evening, as even in my*

*irregularity, I would never suggest that you write to me*
*by post.*

 *Yours, etc.*

 *Charles Musgrove*

Charlotte had to look away twice and lock her shaking hands together before she could finish the note.

It was—it was fantastical. She must be drunk or dreaming or perhaps lying upon her bed in a hallucinatory fever.

She squealed just once, a surge from the seventeen-year-old Charlotte who had given up on marrying for love over ten years ago.

Then she froze. How far was Mary through the song? Everyone would leave when it was over.

Frantically, Charlotte pulled Mr. Bennet's quill and standish from the corner cupboard. It was a blessing she knew Longbourn like the back of her hand.

She flipped Mr. Musgrove's note over.

*Dear Mr. Musgrove,*

She paused. She did not want to appear managing, but time was short, and he was correct that she could not write to him again unless they were engaged. But they could not be engaged until she broke her engagement with Mr. Collins. The strained sounds of Mary heading into a crescendo made her write on .

*Thank you very much for your note. The idea is not at all repugnant to me, and in fact, makes me very happy.*

*My situation is somewhat delicate, and time is short, so forgive me for being practical. I would hate to put you to any trouble or embarrassment, so if you think it best, I propose the following:*

*You leave Meryton as planned to escort the Misses Elliot to Bath. I will write to Mr. Collins. In perhaps two months, when all is calm, you could visit again, and make your addresses to me at that time, if you still wish it.*

Even as she wrote, Charlotte's stomach clenched. Would he still want her in a few months? In the spring, when he might remember that he could do far better?

Oh, she prayed not. Charlotte screwed up her courage.

*If I have made your visit pleasant, I am glad. You have made my winter the best I ever had. If you replace the word comfort with love, your letter might have been written by me.*

*Charlotte Lucas*

Charlotte felt unworthy writing of love, but on the other hand, as she had told Lizzy, gentlemen often needed more encouragement, not less. He had taken the step of writing to her, and he should not have to do *all* the work.

This brought a burn to her cheeks. She folded the note again, placing her words inside, and folded it once more, to make it a triangle. That way all names were obscured.

The last lingering notes of Mary's sonata sounded through the house while Charlotte pressed a hand to the cold window and then to each cheek, forcing some of the heat down. The landscape was black and white in the moonlight, the wet trees waving gently in the wind.

When Charlotte slipped out the door into the hall, the other guests were also making their way out of the parlor. A footman brought out carriage blankets which had been warmed by the kitchen fire. Alice brought out an armful of bulky greatcoats for the gentlemen and colorful cloaks for the ladies.

It was the work of a moment to give Mr. Musgrove the note as he fetched his beaver-trimmed hat from the side table.

He couldn't read it in the hall, but he immediately flushed. Just the fact that she was giving the note *back* and had not burned it told him what he needed to know.

Charlotte was so nervous, she was not sure if she smiled, but he did. He dipped his head, looking pleased but a little embarrassed. "That's all right then. Indeed. Quite so."

Charlotte smiled then. "Thank you, Mr. Musgrove."

"Oh, no. Nothing to it."

They shared a moment of perfect, quiet understanding and then he was swinging up the step into the Longs' carriage and on his way. A stupidly happy smile was plastered on his face.

# { 21 }

LIZZY STOOD IN THE DOORWAY of Longbourn, watching the several carriages go and waving goodbye. She wrapped her arms around herself and pulled her shawl a little tighter.

She probably ought to find her serviceable cloak, but it wasn't worth the effort for the few extra moments she said goodbye.

Charlotte left with her family, and Mr. Musgrove with the Longs, but Lizzy had hope. She had seen a *moment* between them, smiles and blushes and nervous shifting. It had all the earmarks of a romance.

A giant sigh escaped her.

Her stress slowly bled away. She would *never* matchmake again. It was a horrendous way to spend a few weeks, and it could have gone catastrophically wrong. She was lucky she had not caused pain.

Lizzy shivered. Mr. Bingley's carriage still waited on the gravel drive, but neither he nor Mr. Darcy had come out yet. The coachman sat patiently in the seat, but the fine gray horses stamped and snorted clouds of mist into the cold night air.

Lizzy sighed. It would be just like her mother to somehow trap them longer, just when they were ready to go home and to bed, too. They must be rescued.

Mr. Darcy appeared at her shoulder. "Vickers, walk them for ten minutes more, please."

The coachman tipped his head and shook the reins. "O'course, Mr. Darcy. I won't be far, holler when ready."

Lizzy shivered again and stepped back into the front hall.

Mr. Darcy pulled the large wooden door to close out the cold, but it stuck.

"You have to lift and jerk the handle."

He did, but still the door didn't latch. It bounced against the wood framing and swung out again.

"No, it's—here." Lizzy came close to take the brass handle. She twisted it up, put her shoulder into lifting the door slightly to the right, and then it latched and stayed put.

This left her face to face with Mr. Darcy, who had not stepped out of the way.

She could feel his warmth, only inches from her, and she had to tip her head back to look up at him.

The hall was empty, as the rest of the family and Mr. Bingley were still in the parlor. The servants had disappeared, too.

"The foundation of the house has... shifted," Lizzy said.

"Clearly."

His head began to dip towards her, his eyes not leaving her own.

Lizzy—distracted all evening by Charlotte and Mr. Musgrove—woke to her own concerns as if from a long sleep. She could barely remember what she'd said to him the last two days, except that he had nearly always been at hand. Had this been building? Did she *want* it to? Did she cause it?

She rather thought she did cause it, and that maybe she did want it.

Mr. Darcy was the one who paused. He blinked and stood straight again, compressing his mouth as if in punishment for what he'd almost done.

"A moment, Miss Elizabeth?" he asked.

The library door was to hand, just past the stairs. He pulled it open. She went in first and he followed.

The fire was still burning, and a lamp had been lit on the desk, as if to welcome them. Her father had left out his quill and standish rather haphazardly on the desk.

Mr. Darcy clasped his hands behind his back, and then in front of himself. He was not his usual imperturbable self. His silhouette in front of the fire was tall but less imposing than it used to be.

"Miss Elizabeth, do you—is that anxiety you spoke of still weighing on you?"

"Er...not as much, no. I believe the decision was made."

"Good, I don't want to compete with that distraction. Perhaps I was not perfectly honest with you or myself earlier. My unmade decision *was* causing a certain amount of anxiety. I have, however, also made a decision."

"Yes?"

"I'm speaking, " he clasped his hands behind him again, "of us. I have long admired you, at least as long as Bingley has admired your sister. For various reasons, I put you out of my mind. Those reasons—" He thought of Bingley's words on his pride and arrogance. "Those reasons do not matter. Since my return, I have felt even more strongly. More than admiration, I love you."

Lizzy paled. "Do you?"

"I enjoy your playfulness, your quick mind, and your soft heart. I enjoy spending time with you even when—" He cut himself off again. "Despite distractions and difficulties, I find myself counting time until I can be with you again. When I thought, very briefly, that your letter was true and you thought ill of me, I was very unhappy. I realized I cared far more for your opinion than I realized, and I care for no one's opinion." He smiled. "Of course, I soon realized what your letter was for, but I fancy that only shows that I understand you better than most. I would be honored if you accepted my proposal."

This proposal was so different from Mr. Collins's bumbling speeches as to be indistinguishable as the same species. Though Mr. Darcy spoke well, she could read between the lines of his few aborted sentences. She knew what "reasons" had made him decide to put her out of his mind.

What was more astonishing was that she had been in his mind at all, at that point. Her mind was in a whirl. He had been in her thoughts these past weeks, but was it love? Did she dare trust it?

"Your silence is prolonged," Darcy said. "If you wish me to fill it with more protestations of my desire to marry you, I am happy to do so, but I must point out that your family and my friend may come out at any time." He took an aggravated breath. "I have chosen a poor time to speak, I apologize. We are rushed, and you are tired. Perhaps you would like time to reflect and give me your answer tomorrow."

His disappointment was palpable, and Lizzy did not like it at all. In fact, knowing that she had the power to change his disappointment to joy made her distinctly happy.

"That is both generous and humble—but I do not need further time to reflect. I believe, if you are certain that it is what you wish, that I should like to marry you."

Mr. Darcy exhaled audibly, shoulders relaxing, as if he had been holding his breath. "Truly?"

"Strange though it would have seemed several months ago," Lizzy said, "I believe that we might be well-suited for one another." She laughed breathlessly. "In short, I would be glad to accept your offer."

Lizzy tentatively put her hand on his arm for he seemed to be frozen—and his breath stuttered.

"I—I am glad," he said. "I did not realize I did not know your answer until I began to ask it. Presumptuous of me, Bingley would say, and he would be right. I'm learning to think more clearly."

"I appreciate your effort—particularly, by the way, in warning the neighborhood about Wickham. I did not say thank you for that, when we spoke earlier, which I should have done."

"You're welcome. I hope I won't need such prompting to right action in the future, but I'm glad to know I can count on you to prompt me when needed." He took a step forward and another, until he was face to face with Lizzy again. He brought his hand up to stroke her cheek with his thumb. His eyes fell to her lips. "May I...?"

Lizzy, who'd caught Lydia, Mary, and countless other girls in warm embraces in dark corners, smiled. "Yes."

Darcy kissed her as he'd wanted to since the Netherfield ball... or no, it was before that, probably the first time she'd laughed and turned away from him.

Her hair was smooth and warm under his hand. He felt her smile, and his lips followed of their own accord.

They did not hear the door open, but when a female gasp sounded, Darcy jerked away. His hand came to his straighten his cravat, not that it was crooked, and he stood to his full height.

Lizzy pressed a hand to her mouth, though her eyes were laughing.

Lydia, the youngest Bennet girl, stared at them. Then she crowed. "Ha! Now you cannot scold me for kissing under the stairs, for here you are in Papa's *library*! I cannot believe you, Lizzy. Such hypocritism!"

"The word is hypocrisy," Lizzy said, looking quickly at Darcy. "And it isn't, because... Oh, please take yourself off, Lydia. For once."

"Well, I shall, but you owe me."

The door closed, and Lizzy reached for Darcy's hand. "I probably do owe her. You look most forbidding. Your stern face has slammed down so quickly *I* am almost intimidated."

"I am not angry—just embarrassed."

"Don't be. Lydia has no standing to judge anyone. Should we... inform my father? It is rather late—goodness, it must be nearly midnight."

"It *is* late." He swayed half a step towards her, and Lizzy felt a shiver at the longing on his face.

Unfortunately, they both heard the voices of the family in the hallway. Mr. Darcy raised her hand and kissed it.

"If you don't mind," he said, "I think I will call on your father tomorrow."

"Yes, please."

"Until tomorrow then, my dear Elizabeth."

ONDAY BROUGHT MR. MUSGROVE in smiling good humor to pick up Anne and Mary Elliot in his carriage.

Mrs. Long had provided a box of salted pork, bread, and grapes for their journey. Two hot bricks were ready for the ladies, and several carriage blankets were washed, folded, and waiting on the reverse seat.

Anne had seen to it that she and Mary were packed in good time, so there was not much delay except to load their shared trunk and various hatboxes and valises to the rear and top of the carriage.

The day began with a light, spitting rain, and so the Lucas family and the Elliots waited in the drafty but protected foyer of Lucas Lodge for the final goodbye.

Mr. Musgrove found himself grinning at Charlotte, who smiled back at him. At first her smile was tentative, but as she saw that he was his jovial self, even perhaps a bit more lively than usual, her smile became genuine.

Mr. Musgrove had not been at all put out by Charlotte's practical note, though the last line had rather thrilled him. To think that he: commonplace, *ordinary* Charles Musgrove, should inspire a lady with love was quite amazing. He didn't fancy himself a vain man, but there was a special feeling in knowing one was wanted.

And as far as Charlotte's suggested schedule, he could not have agreed more. He appreciated that she took charge of the planning and timing, as it saved much uncertainty and awkward conversation before he left. He was rather used to his mother managing things, and he had perhaps grown a little too used to the women in his life making the day-to-day decisions.

Either way, he considered things all but settled with the least possible fuss and the best possible outcome. What was there not to smile at?

ANNE ELLIOT COULD ONLY WISH the last moments of goodbye over. She had a throbbing headache, probably from lack of sleep.

Mary's unusual cheer and bold words the night before had acted powerfully on Anne. She had been unable to fall asleep until she had put on her dressing gown, gone to Mary's room, and climbed into bed beside her.

Mary could not very well run away without Anne knowing about it if Anne was in the same bed.

Mary, however, was a terrible bedmate. Having never shared with her sisters or her mother as Anne had sometimes done, she elbowed, tugged, and kicked.

Anne's night was most unpleasant. When she woke up for good, Mary had been full of amusement.

"You look absolutely terrible," Mary said. "Your eyes are rimmed in red, and your face has no color, but it is your own fault! I, run away? I am far too smart for that. You have been a busybody, and you have gained a just reward for it."

Maybe Mary was right about that. In the cloudy light of morning, Anne thought perhaps she'd been overwrought and put too much weight on Mary's odd behavior.

Anne could not wait to get to Bath, which was not something she ever expected to say. She hated Bath, as it represented a time of terrible depression after her mother died and an unpleasant interlude after she'd sent Captain Wentworth away.

But this time, at least Bath would mean taking Mary away from Wickham.

Mary Elliot smiled upon all, not even complaining when Charles Musgrove trod on her slipper as he led her to the carriage. He was a great oaf, so prosaic and round. His breath smelled of bacon this morning, and his cheeks were so red.

To think she would probably have married him if he'd asked! Now that she was engaged to her dashing, handsome Wickham, it seemed unthinkable.

Wickham was witty and clever. He was trim and handsome. He was bold and modern.

Also, he was poor, but that only meant he would appreciate her all the more. Mary was tired of being the youngest, the least important, the hanger-on. It was an *honor* for Wickham to marry into the Elliot family and fortune, and she was the one who got to bestow that honor.

Wickham had lost a little shine when he balked at her plans for Bath, but Mary was confident a little resolution would carry the day. He did not know her father as she did, and perhaps he did not like to be painted in a bad light, but if it led to marriage, what was the problem? No, she would do what was best for her and for Wickham, and he couldn't do anything about it.

After all, he'd already asked her to marry him.

WICKHAM ALSO HAD A BAD NIGHT, though not in so selfless a fashion as Anne Elliot.

It had begun with a late evening visit from Colonel Forster. He had heard Wickham's debts being discussed by some of the other young officers. They had been a bit amused at Wickham's sudden descent into *persona non grata* in Meryton. They weren't entirely unsympathetic, but young men could make a jest out of anything.

Colonel Forster was concerned, he'd told Wickham, and thought he might need "a reminder of the behavior expected of an officer of His Majesty's Army."

"It's not the high village debts," Colonel Forster said, "I don't care much about that. But these debts of honor are another thing. I made a few inquiries, and word is you're precious close to reneging."

"I would never do so! How dare they say such things?"

Colonel Forster raised an experienced eyebrow. "Very well, don't tell me. I know how these things go. Just know that you can't go on this way. The honor of the regiment is my honor as well. I also heard there might be a dalliance with the Elliot girl." He shook his head. "Have your fun in safe places, and don't seduce ladies of quality."

Wickham laid a hand on his heart. "I am a man of honor—"

Colonel Forster rose, cutting him off. "Yes, you're a good dramatist, I'm realizing. Take my warning seriously, Wickham. Good evening."

Darcy was the problem behind all of this, and it absolutely burned Wickham that he could do nothing to make him pay. Marrying Georgiana would have been the perfect solution, but Darcy had ruined that, too.

Georgiana was much nicer than Mary Elliot. She did not constantly fancy herself ill-used. She was flattered with his attention, rather than demanding. And she had certainly never threatened to tell tales of him to her father!

Mary's ultimatum was simple. He must go to Bath and court her properly, or she would tell her father he'd compromised her. It was ridiculous. For one thing, he *hadn't* compromised her, and it was most unjust to use that as a threat when he hadn't even gotten to enjoy it.

For another, a woman should shy away from such claims, not use them as bludgeons.

Wickham flopped on his bed—narrow and hard— and grabbed the tobacco pouch on the water stand. He packed tobacco into his pipe, tamping it down, and using the candle to light it.

This called for a smoke.

Would Mary's plan work? Her father would not want to spread the tale abroad. Much as Darcy had hushed up Georgiana's "indiscretion," Sir Walter would probably do likewise. That could go badly for Wickham.

Sir Walter didn't seem the dueling type, but then... he could definitely speak to Colonel Forster and that would be bad.

One way or another, Wickham's time with the army was burnt to the socket.

He cursed.

He grabbed a dirty glass, rubbed it on the blanket on the bed, and poured two fingers of whiskey.

His first option was to abandon Mary and disappear. Start again in London or some other watering hole. But he had not much to live on, and dash it—a man must live on something. Wickham would never submit to menial labor, but the options of genteel work were limited.

His other option was to go to Bath and see if Mary could push her father to allow their marriage. She did seem determined. It annoyed him, but he also understood her. Wickham was willing to do anything for his aims, and so was she.

With a grim smile, Wickham raised his whiskey to her and downed it. Bath, it was. Darned if he wouldn't make Mary pay for this.

He left in the morning, debts unpaid due to insolvency, and with a burning sense of righteous indignation.

AT LONGBOURN, OVER A LATE breakfast of sweet buns, boiled eggs, and cold pork—left from the roasted ham the previous night—Lizzy spread her hands flat on the table.

"I have a piece of news."

Mrs. Bennet was sipping a cup of weak tea with half-closed eyelids. Her hair was still in loose, wavy tangles, and she wore her dressing gown. "Oh, yes?"

"Is it about last night?" Lydia said. "Because if so, I have news to share also. I caught Lizzy and Mr. Darcy—"

"Lydia! Let me finish."

Mrs. Bennet sniffed. "Lydia, my dear, I know Lizzy and Mr. Darcy were together a large part of Sunday, but that was because I was trying to give Mr. Bingley time with Jane."

"Mother," Jane protested.

"Do not mother at me—it worked!" Mrs. Bennet sighed happily. "You girls do not appreciate my efforts, but I am resigned to a thankless task."

Lizzy tried again. "Mr. Darcy spoke to me last night."

"He spoke to me also," said Lizzy's father, looking up from the London newspaper. "Sensible man. I saw him eyeing my copy of *Schematicas,* and I asked him if he knew it. He said, 'Not at all. The binding is eye-catchingly ugly.'" Mr. Bennet chuckled. "It is, too. I usually have my books bound by Tate, but this one I bought through your uncle in London. Puce and pink."

Mrs. Bennet frowned. "He ought not insult your books, Mr. Bennet! Mr. Darcy is a very strange man, and I cannot decide if I like him. First he was rude to you, Lizzy, which I cannot at all like when he did not even bother to praise Jane. Then Wickham told such stories about him! But breeding will out, and no one worth as much as Mr. Darcy could be all bad, could he? Toplofty, yes. I do not at all approve of insulting a neighbor's books."

"Speaking of books," Lydia began.

"He proposed," Lizzy blurted out. "If all of you would stop for a moment, I am trying to explain that Mr. Darcy offered for me, and I accepted. He will call on you later today, Papa."

The silence was broken by Lydia. "And *I* caught them kissing in the library."

Her desire to shock the family fell flat, for they were already shocked. Lydia crossed her arms and huffed. "Lizzy lectures me about propriety, but no one cares that Lizzy was being indiscreet among Papa's books!"

Mr. Bennet's paper was frozen halfway to the table. "Ah. My library seems to have seen of all sorts of use yesterday. My lamp was left burning, my ink was dry. Perhaps I should have a lock installed."

"Mr. Bennet! Is that all you can say?" demanded Mrs. Bennet. "Lizzy will be *Mrs. Darcy*! Oh, I have never loved a gentleman better! He is so witty and dry! I knew it all when Alice told me he walked Lizzy to the apothecary. I told you all, I said, 'That *means* something.'"

"Eloquent and prophetic, my dear."

"Yes! Ten thousand pounds a year in interest! What carriages you will have, what finery, what allowance!"

Lizzy grimaced. "He greatly dislikes having it spoken of."

"Oh, I know! As if I should be *gauche* enough to refer to a man's fortune! You give me no credit at all, Lizzy."

"Yes, ma'am."

"He kissed you?" Kitty asked. "He is so stiff!"

"Don't ask improper questions," Jane said, blushing. "Perhaps it is not quite the norm, but they are engaged—"

"Your father snuck a kiss or two during the weeks the banns were read," said Mrs. Bennet, complacent. "I've no complaint as long as they're discreet."

"It was not your library that was violated," Mr. Bennet protested. He frowned at Lizzy. "In all seriousness, is this a good choice? I know you were suspicious of Wickham's claims all along, but that is not the same as wanting to spend your life with Mr. Darcy. Be careful, Lizzy. If you marry someone you don't respect, it will not end well."

"I do respect him."

"He beat her at chess," Mary put in.

"Yes, he is intelligent," Lizzy agreed, "which is important to me. But more than that, he has shown a willingness to listen, to humble himself, and to change. I think those are a solid foundation for respect."

"Humble himself?" Mrs. Bennet sounded as if Lizzy had asked Darcy to shave his head. "Why would you ask him to do that? You are such a strange girl, Lizzy, it is a *miracle* he has asked you! You must try to be more like Jane."

"But he did not ask Jane to marry him," Mr. Bennet answered. "His choice of Lizzy is the best thing I know of him."

"Thank you, Papa."

"Just promise to invite me to the library at Pemberley. All these great houses have them. I doubt as to its being properly stocked or catalogued, but one never knows what one may find, even if it is bound in puce and pink."

Lizzy paled. "I had not thought much about Pemberley."

Their footman appeared at the door. "Mr. Darcy to call on Mr. Bennet, sir."

Mrs. Bennet flew up. "And me in my dressing gown and crumbs all over the table! Hurry, Lizzy, hurry!"

"It's me he's asked to see," said Mr. Bennet.

"But it's Lizzy he *wants* to see; and see her he shall."

*Starch and Strategy*

For once, Lizzy and her mother were in perfect agreement.

# Epilogue

*D*EAR MR. COLLINS,

    *I apologize in advance for the pain this letter may bring you. I have made a mistake, entirely of my own doing, and I have realized that I must dissolve our engagement.*

    *It is the role of a man to ask, and though a bitter thing at times, it is the role of the lady to withdraw. I must do so. The circumstances could only displease you and not absolve me, therefore I will say no more. Please think of me as kindly as you can, and please give my apologies to Lady Catherine. I am fully sensible of the honor you have done me, and the honor she bestowed in giving her approval.*

    *Wishing you all future joy and prosperity, with deepest gratitude,*

    *Charlotte Lucas*

*Miss Lucas,*

*My disapprobation of this turn is extreme! Lady Catherine has said that it is very ill-done of you, and it is only her unparalleled elegance and goodness of heart that prevents her using stronger language. She is greatly displeased; it is not too much to say, disgusted.*

*She has encouraged me to wash my hands of your family, and so I do. If you think to receive me ever again at Lucas Lodge, you are fooling yourself. You pretended to be a sensible and mature woman, but now I see that you are as flighty and untrue as any pretty young girl. I have enclosed a copy of Fordyce's sermon on the topic of False Promises and Flirtation for your edification.*

*Sincerely,*
*Rev. William Collins*

*Dear Caroline,*

*I'm engaged! Darcy said I really must write you. I had rather be with my beautiful Jane this morning, but I see that he is right. It would not do for you to read of this in the newspaper.*

*My dear Jane and I are engaged. You always said she was a sweet girl, so I hope this brings you joy, for I am excessively happy.*

*In other news, Darcy has proposed to Miss Elizabeth Bennet. It did not surprise me, for I was canny and noticed what was in the wind, but I daresay it will surprise many others.*

*Jane and I shall have the banns read and marry in February. You need not come back for the wedding unless you wish.*

*I hope you are having a jolly time in Bath with the Elliots. The younger two went on their way last week, so I suppose they are there.*

*There was some kerfuffle with Wickham and he has disappeared from his regiment, leaving a slew of debt behind. He always was a rotter.*

*Look at that, I have filled up a whole page!*

*Take care,*

*Charles*

Lizzy accompanied Mr. Darcy to Meryton, where he posted a letter to his sister, Georgiana.

"She will be thrilled at this development," he said. "I look forward to introducing you."

"What does she know of me thus far?" Lizzy asked. "What have you written of me?"

He tucked Lizzy's hand further around his arm as they walked toward the south side of town, back toward Longbourn. "Not much, I'm afraid. I felt too deeply to write about it. I believe I mentioned that you play the pianoforte charmingly."

Lizzy's mouth fell open, incredulous. "Of all the strange things—now I believe that you do truly love me, for that is almost a lie."

"It is not."

"Shall I tell you what you *ought* to have written?"

"Certainly."

"You should have said: Dear Georgiana. There is a most impertinent girl here who takes delight in poking fun at me. I would take it amiss, but clearly she is falling for my height and good looks, therefore I will have patience."

Mr. Darcy only smiled at her silliness, though she thought his neck was a trifle flushed. He steadied her as they left the pavement of the town for the overgrown path next to the Lea.

"The next letter," Lizzy continued, "you could have said: Lizzy is distracted by a very unwise plot to help her friend, but I will wait until she is done and surprise her with my proposal. She will be happier than she has ever been, and I will be too, though of course I will not show it on my face."

"Do I not look happy?" he asked. He was smiling now, and even in the dreary December light, Lizzy had never seen him look more handsome.

"Oh, you do! How shall I reward you?"

There was no one in sight, so Lizzy raised up on her toes to kiss his cheek.

Mr. Darcy turned, making it a real kiss, making it last.

Lizzy knew she was red when she pulled away. "Mr. Darcy!"

She took his cold hand and pressed it to her over-warm cheek, first one side, then the other. "You surprised me. You are usually so full of starch and reserve."

"Do you want to know what the last letter would have said?" He leaned close to her. "I've fallen in love with a beautiful woman, and I can hardly wait to bring her home."

Lizzy wiped an unexpected tear from her eye. "Now you have made *my* happiness show all over my face."

They walked back to Longbourn in a cloud of contentment that left all Lizzy's strategies far behind.

# Don't miss Book 2!

## *Propriety and Piquet*
### He's a con artist. She's impossible.

George Wickham has few morals and even fewer scruples. He planned to seduce and marry the youngest Elliot sister, but somehow she has turned the tables on him. Will Mary entrap Wickham before he realizes how their family fortune has dwindled?

Meanwhile, Colonel Fitzwilliam is on duty, tracking down a spy who is leaking information to the French. He won't deny he'd *like* to pin the crime on Wickham, but he suspects someone more respectable is the villain. Perhaps even someone in the Elliot family.

And poor Anne Elliot is trapped at Bath with a growing vision of the catastrophes about to befall her family. If Captain Wentworth were to return now, he would find the Elliot family in complete turmoil.

## About the Author

Corrie Garrett is a Christian author of romance, fantasy, and sci-fi. She lives and works in the beautiful hills of West Virginia, with her husband, four kids, and a rather hard-headed blue heeler.

86624010R00187